PARANORMAL BONDS

THE HIGH COUNCIL WITCH CHRONICLES

JULIE CATHERINE

PARANORMAL BONDS

THE HIGH COUNCIL WITCH CHRONICLES, BOOK 1

JULIE CATHERINE

Edited by
KATIE WOLF

For Bub and little Bub

CONTENTS

ONE
WELCOME TO PLUMPKIN

"OH MY GOD. What are you doing?!"

I stepped out of the room just long enough to wash my hands with the yummy peppermint soap in the hallway bathroom instead of the lemon cleaner by the sink, and by the time I returned, Aunt Abeline had stacked seventeen plates and a bottle of ketchup into her arms. She was gingerly making her way from our counter to the table.

"I used to be a waitress," she claimed, her thumb in the salad.

I swooped in and took the most breakable items away.

We settled them all on the table, careful not to disturb the never-ending Scrabble game. The slab was filled with knives, forks, glasses, plates, trivets, and, of course, a piping hot pot of creamy cheese pasta. My favorite.

"Nothing to fear," she said with a little wiggle.

"Uh-huh..."

I breathed a sigh of relief as we pulled out our regular chairs. In a million years, I would have never attempted anything so careless. Aunt Abeline would have had my head. But when she took a foolish risk, it was ditzy and cute. Not that I'd point out the discrepancy. These little criticisms lived and died in my head. I didn't even roll my eyes.

"Ooh, you added bacon," I realized.

"I did."

Aunt Abeline put her paper towel in her lap like a proper cloth napkin.

"Why?" I eyed her nervously. "What's wrong?"

I scooped a serving onto each of our plates but eyed my dinner companion.

"Nothing's wrong. Can't an aunt make her niece's favorite dish for no reason?"

"She can..."

I waited.

Aunt Abeline didn't meet my eyeline. Her thin fingers snatched up the pepper grinder and twisted delicious flavor over her moon-shaped noodles. I nudged my meal towards her, and she added three twists of seasoning over my dish as well. She still hadn't glanced at my face. That wasn't a good sign.

So I waited.

The pasta gave off an aroma of sticky, hot deliciousness, but I didn't succumb to the allure of the carbs. Not yet anyway.

I could wait all day.

"Oh, alright. We need to stay a little while. Salt?"

"The bacon's already salty."

We both knew she couldn't derail me that quickly.

"Stay? Here?" I asked.

"Mm-hmm."

"At the lake house?"

"Right."

She let the information settle by making a show of looking at our board game.

"*Squeeze* was such a good word," she said, complimenting my playing. "It's rare, you know, to use multiple high value letters in a bingo. And to make my word plural as well... you've gotten much better."

For once, I was beating her score. We both knew it wouldn't last.

I frowned.

"Don't change the subject."

"It's nice here. Don't you like it?" She smiled. "I do."

Oof. The discussion was over before it began. We were staying.

"I like to visit," I agreed.

We had been coming to this little lakeside cabin for a weekend here, a week or two there since before I could remember.

"But to live? Permanently?"

I frowned and looked out the window at the overgrown branches.

Our little house was the eighth property on a low traffic street that covered one corner of the lake.

Beyond us, there were four other houses until you hit the dead end. All the residents on the street were seasonal cottage owners, like me and my aunt. It was a great hideaway. The local highway was hidden from view on the other side of the forest, and when you sat with your feet up by the lake, the rest of the world seemed a million miles away.

It was the perfect spot for a vacation.

From the deck, all you could see were the trees, the sun-dappled water, and maybe a woodland friend scampering from one hideaway to another.

You came to a place like this to get away from it all...

What would life be like if this was all you had?

Plumpkin, town of 4,000.

Now 4,002, I guessed.

"What about the condo?"

"It's a sublet." She shrugged.

She'd simply get rid of it, like we'd shed so many other residences.

I forced down a couple nibbles.

"Alright," I said.

My aunt had relocated us more times than I could remember, so this impromptu decision was surprising, but not really a shock. In fact, it would be far bigger news if we lasted a whole year in one location. But the apartments that we filled with hand-me-down furniture and then sold out on auction sites were usually in big cities, with traffic cameras and sky-rises and homeless beggars you'd avoid or befriend.

When we didn't move to cities, we lived in smaller suburbs, with big box stores and dying downtown strips that had been overtaken by corporate coffee shops and condo-townhouses on every second block.

I never considered we'd cross the threshold into living in a tiny, tiny town.

And Plumpkin was barely that.

The whole population seemed smaller than my last high school.

Besides, we'd had plenty of opportunities to make this place home.

Little that I knew about the whole family's history, the Kingsley cottage lore was fairly well known. My mom's side bought the property when it was still a blank parcel. Grandma Mim and Grandpa Charles fell in love with the calming, peaceful waters and the obscenely cheap price for a waterfront lot. They built every square inch of the building from the ground up, even laid their own plumbing. The home would stay in the bloodline as a piece of family heritage passed from generation to generation until the day we all died.

The shoddy workmanship and rustic furniture choices of the cabin were considered quaint, even special. The uncomfortable, non-matching couches held every butt in the family. Modern, or designer, or stylish they were not.

But that was fine. After all, it was a cottage.

Every year, we rolled in on hot, sunny weekends with the rest of the out-of-towners. My aunt and I would arrive on a Friday, enjoy the fresh off-the-water breeze, get our holiday groceries from the local Jug City, and have a couple great days going for canoe rides, swatting overzealous mosquitoes, and eating campfire s'mores. Then on Sundays, we'd roll back to the hot pavement traffic jam of real life.

To me, that was Plumpkin.

I knew each of the hiking trails and all the best flavors at the local ice cream store. It was a cute place to visit. But that didn't mean I wanted to stay.

I managed half my dinner, then wrapped the other side for later.

We had plenty of leftovers. But I just couldn't eat.

"I think you'll like going to school here," Aunt Abeline offered. "You know, your mom and I went to Plumpkin High."

I almost coughed into the napkin I was using to dab my mouth dry.

"Really?" I leaned forward.

We'd long left this subject, but never landed firm on another topic.

I just couldn't muster the effort. That's what our Scrabble game was for.

The safety of wordsmithing.

But Aunt Abeline must have been feeling especially guilty about this latest relocation, because this new piece of info she dropped was big news.

Huge.

"For a couple semesters." She nodded. "We did."

We never spoke about Sierra.

Never.

A million questions rushed to my mind, but I was careful.

I didn't want to spook her.

The door had cracked open, but if I pushed too far or too fast, Aunt Abeline would slam it shut once more.

I'd been down this road too many times. I was hungry for any detail about my mom that I could muster but I knew the rejection would come ruthless and swift if my desperation showed. Aunt Abeline would claim that I still wasn't ready. But not if I walked on a very fine line.

I settled on asking something open-ended but impersonal.

"So you grew up in this town?"

"We moved around a lot. You knew that."

Oops, a dead end.

My aunt stood and gathered the dishes. She seemed to regret having opened the door. Her efficient hands snagged each item and moved them back to their homes on the shelves.

I needed a new track.

Fast.

I stood and helped her. Sliding all the porcelain and glass into the machine to be washed.

"Sure," I agreed, trying to keep the conversation going.

Soon, the supper would be put away.

When the dinner was gone, so would be my window.

I was losing my chance.

"Okay. Well, tell me about the teachers," I said.

I tried a new tactic but, being so wrapped up in my words, I didn't watch where I was going. The bottle of ketchup in my hands tilted and fell to its side. It clattered on the counter.

"Sorry. Nothing spilled, don't worry." I recovered quickly, but the damage was done.

Aunt Abeline *tut-tutted*. She closed the refrigerator with our leftovers inside.

"You can't control what happens, Mae. Summer goes, then seasons change. It's your reaction that matters. You know that." She gave a little frown, then retired down the hall to her bedroom.

"Oh, I know," I murmured when I was sure she wouldn't hear. "I know all too well."

I sighed and resigned myself to scrub our pasta pot.

It felt good to sink my hands in the hot, soapy water.

I was silly for getting my hopes up.

The pan washed up easily. So I folded the dish towel and slid the thin fabric on the rail in front of the stove. Aunt Abeline thought I wasn't old enough to learn the family secrets. I wasn't responsible enough to know the details. But at least I'd learned something.

Mom had lived at the lake house.

Well, of course.

I think I'd always known she must have stayed in this place for a while.

Logistically, that was a reasonable assumption. I'm not sure why I hadn't considered it before.

This was the family's cottage.

We were sharing the same four wallpapered walls, the same wooden door. Maybe even the same lumpy bed.

Which room had been hers?

The one I now used, or the guest room down the hall?

I wandered to the back half of the cottage and slipped into my bedroom, shutting the door behind me.

Our bedroom.

This was the room Sierra would have picked. I knew deep inside.

The light here was better, and the window overlooked the water.

I took a small pocketknife out of the interior pouch in my backpack and clicked it open. I sunk down in the space between the door and the dresser, stretching my legs out in front of me, careful not to get nicked by the little blade. For a moment, I examined its sharp angles, then I used the knife to create a thin slice in the bottom side of the door, right near the hinge. Just a tiny gouge. Nothing Aunt Abeline would notice. I did this in the bedroom of every home I ever lived in. A little physical reminder that I was there.

I'd come and gone.

A tiny mark to make a house a home.

Plumpkin was now our home.

First Mom's, and now mine.

I closed the knife and pulled out the bottom drawer

near my butt. I plopped the blade inside and swept the furniture closed. I looked at my carved handiwork. My fingers traced the knick. For a moment, I let myself go, losing my thoughts in the simple, tactile feeling. Its presence brought me comfort. I didn't have much, but in every place that we ever moved I always had that mark. One little divot. No matter what life's curves might throw me, I could always close my doorway and return to that corner.

I was there.

This was home.

Aunt Abeline didn't have to know.

"Your turn," she called through the closed door. Her voice was gentle, not to disturb me, but also surprisingly loud. She was unaware I was sitting only inches behind the plywood.

"What'd you play?" I asked, not bothering to breach my four walls.

"*Zymurgy.*"

I waited.

"Do you know what it means?"

"You know I don't."

"How would I possibly know which words you do or don't know?" she complained, but I could tell she was incredibly pleased with herself.

"The fermentation process of wine or beer," she said.

I could almost hear her smile through the wood.

She loved to define her latest Scrabble word. Maybe more than she liked the actual game itself. She couldn't care less about winning. Mostly because with me as her only opponent, she had yet to lose a game.

"Right. Zymurgy." I rolled my eyes. "I'd still like to hear more about your high school experience," I added, cocking my head. A half-hearted Hail Mary.

I could almost hear her happiness wither.

"Of course, dear. We'll talk tomorrow."

Aunt Abeline spiked the inquiry to the floor.

I listened to the telltale sounds of her shuffling away and settling down the hall with a good book and a hot cup of tea.

She was right.

We would talk tomorrow.

And the next day.

And every day after that.

But not about her schooling.

Not about Mom.

Not even about the choice to relocate.

That decision had been made.

The moment was over and done with.

Aunt Abeline and I were here to stay.

TWO
WAKING UP IN PLUMPKIN

WAKING up in Plumpkin the next morning felt totally different than it had even one day ago. I was no longer a tourist. Each nook and crack of the cabin was my permanent residence. Like the mouse deterrent buzzer humming quietly in the outlet near the dresser. How had I never noticed it before?

Did we have a rodent problem?

The little whir of the motor was super annoying.

Would the issue get worse as the weather got colder? There were answers to these questions that I didn't want to find out.

"I'll head back to the city this weekend to pack up the rest of our belongings," Aunt Abeline told me over breakfast.

I stood over the sink eating a buttered piece of toast that was dark brown and crispy. I always popped the hammer back down to get the bread slice to its crunchiest, duskiest color content only moments before it burned. My timing was impeccable.

"Anyone you wanna say goodbye to?"

"Nah. I'm good." I shrugged, catching the crumbs as I took another bite. Little toasty morsels rained down into the sink below. A few crumbs tumbled into my clothes. I wiggled, trying to catch them as they tickled against my skin.

"Oh... alright."

Aunt Abeline nodded, but I could tell my lack of friends made her a little sad.

That's what happened when you moved around a lot.

We'd only been at the last sublet for three months. Just long enough to pass my spring courses. I knew a bunch of kids' names from some boring group projects, and I followed their social media stuff. They were nice and all, but I didn't really like any of them, and none of them really liked me. We didn't connect or interact in a way that was meaningful.

And that was fine.

If I never returned to that school, no one would be sad.

Including me.

It was what it was.

When I was younger, I had left other homes in a wake of sorrow, but after a few awful farewells, you learn to keep your feelings at bay. Now I just coasted. Minded my business. Gave the people what they wanted. Stayed super quiet. Sometimes it was just easier to remain anonymous.

"Use a plate, dear."

"Right, of course." I grabbed a saucer from the dish rack and hovered over it with the remaining crusts. "I'll come help." I nodded.

"No need, I'll be done in a jiff. Why don't you go exploring?"

"I haven't done that since I was a little girl."

"You're still young," she said with a sad smile.

To myself, I just rolled my eyes.

"Well, alright. If we're going to live here for a while, I better learn all I can about this..." I trailed off. *Dump*, I wanted to add, but I didn't have the nerve. Instead, the end of the sentence just hung in the air.

Plumpkin *was* a bit dumpy.

I grew up on pristine streets lined with bespoke shops, fancy stores, hole-in-the-wall restaurants, and delicious eateries. I grew up in malls, trolling the food courts, faced with hundreds of culinary choices, each selection cheaper and bigger and saltier and sweeter. I grew up in ethnic communities with a thousand little diners, was served the best authentic dishes by wrinkled men and women who would talk about you right in front of you, to your face, in languages you didn't understand.

What was so great about Plumpkin?

It had a farmers market, a diner, two independently owned coffee shops on Main Street, and one fancy golf course restaurant that required reservations if you didn't want to sit at the bar. The stores on the strip were mediocre tourist traps with handwoven, overpriced clothing, magnets, knickknacks, and crap.

At least I could order whatever I actually wanted over the Internet.

"There's a roof overhead," Aunt Abeline said. "What more do you need?"

Some information about my mother would be nice, I thought to myself, but said nothing. I would never get anything more by attacking the source.

"I remember this one summer..." She rolled into the story of the season she'd spent living in a converted motorhome, skipping out on paying rent for a four week period.

I pretended to listen.

Spending a month in her car didn't make her a bohemian any more than moving to Plumpkin for part or all of this semester would make me a townie. When I heard a pause in her story, I made a break for the front porch and wandered away from the house over to the garage shed.

I looked back at our new home and caught sight of Aunt Abeline puttering in the kitchen. She seemed so happy and calm.

How could I get through to her it was time to let me in on the *real* material?

The weather was just starting to show signs of the summer's end and the quick descent into winter that would follow on the heels of the fall. But it would hold itself together for today's little adventure, I felt certain. I hopped on my bike and rode down onto Main Street. I trekked from one end of town to the other in exactly four minutes. After completing that circuit, I headed for the one place my aunt and I had never ventured before. On all of our many summer visits, it was the one place we'd never bothered to go: the school.

The high school my teenage mom had attended.

Plumpkin High.

The school was on a separate street from its neighbors.

Compared to the rest of the community, the school was too large, a reflection of poor urban planning. Once, the institute had been the only school for an hour plus drive in any direction. Kids were bussed in from all over. During its heyday, Plumpkin High burst at the seams. Local councils had demanded something be done to alleviate overcrowding, so two nearby counties built not one, but two new academic buildings to diversify the spread of kids. I guess they thought the local townspeople would just keep popping out more babies, but instead, it drastically divided the school population into thirds. The neighboring kids were shipped off to new buildings that were closer in distance. There simply weren't enough students in the county to fill the three separate schools. Rather than admit their mistake, the politicians ignored the issue, doubling down with longer bus routes and larger catchment areas until all three buildings had just enough kids to justify their existence. They each ran year after year with tiny populations that couldn't possibly be covered by the local taxpayer funds.

Today, the grounds were empty.

Still summer for another week, their appearance was gaunt and forgotten. But there was some movement as the staff began getting ready for the new season. In the back field, a custodian rode a motorized vehicle to cut the large, grassy lawn.

I wondered how my mom had felt when she'd attended.

Did she know how backwater and tiny this school really was? Had she been scholastically inclined? Did she ever have to worry about a shady reputation? Was she a part of any teams or clubs?

I rolled right up to the front doors and tried to get in the building. Locked. I leaned close to the window and shielded the reflection, looking inside. I wondered if I'd find pictures of my mom and aunt in the compilations of graduating students. Most schools lined photos from the past in their atrium halls. I tried to peek inside.

"It's not so bad."

I whipped around to see a handsome boy leaning out his driver's side window. He was watching me, grinning. His vehicle had to be some green energy, whisper-quiet thing because a moment earlier, I was certain that I had been alone.

"Didn't mean to scare you," he added, but the twinkle in his eye proved otherwise.

"You didn't," I replied, holding my head high, hiding my jumpy feelings.

"You registering this year?"

"Yeah."

Years ago, I had taken over all the form filing and official mumbo jumbo paperwork. We moved so often I had it down to a science, knowing exactly what the school administrators would want. All my aunt had to do was sign it. Last night, I updated my paperwork and prepared it all in triplicate. But I wasn't about to tell him all that.

His arm was surprisingly muscular. Maybe it was the way he was leaning out of the car a little, but his forearm had a crease that alluded to the strength and agility of an athlete and a tan that implied a leisurely season of swimming and sun.

Plus, he had his own car.

A new car.

His family had money.

Aunt Abeline had always valued her time and freedom far more than any trinkets a big payday could provide. She expected me to do the same.

He nodded. "Your tire is flat."

I looked down at my wheel, then back to his car, but he was already driving away.

He gave a little wave out the window, then he was gone.

"Thanks... for nothing."

I climbed out from my straddle and checked out the frame. He was right. The back tire was a total pancake. So much for my little ride about town.

I considered calling Aunt Abeline. She would definitely come pick me up, but I didn't want her to question how I got the flat. I didn't really have an answer, and I didn't want her to think I was any less responsible than she already did. Especially now, with the new Sierra-bomb that was ticking. My mom, at my school. All the potential new information just waiting to be discovered. I wanted to prove I could handle myself.

I was an adult. I would do my own rescuing.

Of course, had the dude who pointed out my flat tire been even a teensy bit of a gentleman and offered me a lift to the nearest gas station, I wouldn't have needed rescuing at all.

But he didn't.

And truthfully, if he had, I probably wouldn't have gone. Who gets in the car with some strange... handsome guy?

I grinned to myself.

Yeah, he was kind of good-looking.

Rich and hot.

Maybe there'd be more guys like him and Plumpkin wouldn't be such a bad little town after all.

I tested the bike frame.

Without my extra weight, the pancake tire rolled along fine, so although I couldn't ride it, I could travel along beside it.

It was going to be a long, slow walk home.

But then, I almost laughed. Because it didn't matter if it was a long and lonely stroll.

I had nowhere else to be.

I had nowhere else to go.

THREE
THE FIRST DAY

I TOOK my time unpacking the boxes that Aunt Abeline returned with from the city. Neither she nor I were big on possessions, in part because everything we owned, so many times for the convenience of relocating, had been bought and sold.

My clothing filled the dresser and the little closet in the corner of my bedroom. My neutrals and understated colors all hung in a row. It was the first time in Plumpkin I'd ever had to worry about my wardrobe. I spent most of my tourist weekends and hot summer days in a cover-up or swimsuit, not exactly socially presentable. So when the first day of school arrived, I was a little bit nervous about the suitability of my clothes.

Kids could be awful about the smallest things, like the wrong shoes or an out of place sweater, and I was a long way from the places I'd previously called home.

I hoped the vibe here was casual.

To be safe, I dressed in the most benign pieces of clothing I owned: jean shorts and a white T-shirt. I added a little makeup to my freshly scrubbed face: just some black mascara and a touch of eyeliner on the outer corner of my top lids. I threw my hair in a messy bun and to elevate the look just a bit I added some jewelry. At the base of my calf, I clasped my favorite anklet, a necklace with a full moon charm, hanging just above my foot.

The chain was long enough to wear around your neck and that's how it was originally intended, but when I doubled it over, it wrapped itself to the perfect length around the delicate bones of my ankle. I thought it looked both subtle and sophisticated. Just a touch of sparkle. I would be fresh meat at the school, I knew, so everything had to be perfect. This wasn't my first school transfer with Aunt Abeline, and it likely wouldn't be my last. By now I was used to the drill. All eyes would be on me, so my goal for the next few days was to become as unobjectionable as possible. If I did my job right, I would practically disappear from view.

Of course, fading into the crowd might not be easy in a town of 4,002.

Aunt Abeline tried not to look interested as I walked into the kitchen but failed miserably. I clocked her watching me four times while I buttered my toast.

"What?" I asked finally, my mouth full of grains.

"You look nice."

She grinned immediately, giving up the ruse.

"Thanks," I said, swallowing too much in one mouthful.

I dusted the extra crumbs from my hands into the sink.

"Excited for the new school?"

"No." I laughed.

Aunt Abeline smiled too.

"Well, they'll be excited to have you."

I just nodded.

Sure they would.

"Maybe at this one... try to make a couple friends," she suggested carefully.

I nodded again, moving on to my second piece of toast.

"Is that Grandma's necklace?"

I was surprised that she'd noticed.

I looked down at my ankle. The thin double chain with the tiny moon charm dangled at a pleasing angle. It was the moon that made the bangle so unique. The shape was a complete circle, a full moon whose shadows and etchings, in the right light, could also look like the outline of a crescent. So many cheap jewelry store charms depicted the sun's partner in a one-dimensional slice, but the view of this charm was constantly changing, just as our view of the real moon would change as it rotated the earth. It made the piece feel more expensive, but I'd never thought of it as a family heirloom. It was mine, and before that my mom's, and before that, I guess it was her mom's too. That made it Grandma Mim's necklace. When I framed it like that, was it too valuable to wear near my foot? I didn't want to insult my aunt, but I also didn't want to take it off. The jewelry completed my outfit. It's what took the look from basic to effortlessly styled.

Cautiously, I nodded.

I'd worn it as an anklet many times before and Aunt Abeline had never seemed to notice. What made this time any different?

I eyed her and crossed my legs protectively.

"She'd be glad to know that you're wearing it," my aunt said.

Did she just get teary-eyed?

"I'll be careful," I told her. She nodded.

"First day! This is momentous. Let's get a picture of you."

Abruptly, Aunt Abeline pushed back from her chair. "

Where's my phone?"

She hurried out of the room, but I caught sight of her shadow in the hall, wiping away the wetness around her eyes.

Weird.

It wasn't like her to get so emotional.

I shoveled the last bit of toast in my mouth, but now that she'd brought my attention to it, I looked down at the delicate chains. Maybe the charm held more meaning than I'd thought. I never knew my grandma. Mim and Charles were both gone before I was born.

I'd seen pictures, of course.

They were a striking couple, and she was a beautiful woman with amazing posture. A total class act. At least, that's how she looked. I'm sure that's where Aunt Abeline learned her prim and proper demeanor. If she'd still been alive, I wondered what she'd say about my casually curated, messy choices.

I blasted my butter knife with a shot of hot water in the sink and then stuffed the cutlery into the dishwasher below.

"Smile!"

Aunt Abeline had found her phone and returned as my personal paparazzi.

I gave her a bemused look and a raised eyebrow.

"Is that how you want to be remembered for all eternity?" she said disapprovingly.

I scrunched up my nose and made a sillier face in reply.

"My darling, it's your first day of school in a new, magical place. Let me document the moment like a good auntie. You'll thank me later."

I thought again of the poses of Grandma Mim in old photos. Aunt Abeline was right. The pictures gave the tiniest taste of the woman she was. I straightened up and smiled for the camera.

"That's better."

Aunt Abeline snapped her photos, then looked out from the camera.

"Maybe a little lip gloss? We want to look our best."

"What are you, my stylist?" I complained, but I

dug a pot of pink lip gloss out of my pocket and raked the shine across my bottom lip.

I let her take one more photo.

"I'm going to be late for the bus."

With my bike tire still flat, I had no choice but to take the big yellow school transit.

Looking ahead, if Aunt Abeline and I were going to journey out the rest of my high school career in these backwoods, we would need to seriously look into getting me a car.

But today, I was at the collective whim of the local passengers and driver.

I grabbed my bag, blowing by her.

Since our road was a dead-end, I had to jog down the lane to my stop.

"Call if you get in any trouble," Aunt Abeline said as the screen porch door banged closed behind me.

I rolled my eyes.

It was high school.

How much trouble could there be?

FOUR

TWO VERY DIFFERENT WOMEN

DOWN THE ROAD, I didn't have to wait long for the bus. In fact, if Aunt Abeline had gotten even one more photo, I might have missed it. The big yellow transit took up the whole side of the road where the lane forked from the other Lake Abernathy residential road on the south shore and curved back through our small forest up to the main highway. The driver stopped without pulling over on the shoulder, pumped her flashing lights, and threw open the folding door. If any other driver was in a hurry in front or behind her, they would have to try their hand at off-roading to get past on the road. But legally, they weren't allowed to. That was the power of the school bus zone.

"Name?"

The woman barely looked up from her checklist as I boarded.

"Mae Kingsley."

She cross-checked me against her kid catalog and

then waved me onboard. She tossed the clipboard on the dashboard in front of her and cranked the doors closed behind me.

I climbed the bus steps and looked at my seating choices.

The front bus stalls were empty.

No one ever sat there unless they absolutely had to.

In too-close proximity to the driver, you'd be exposed to the entrance and exits of all your fellow students.

The middle seats were usually the safest. With wall-to-wall windows surrounding you, the sturdy, eye-height fabric lining the seat backs of the middle partitions made the occupants feel camouflaged. If you sat low on the benches, you could barely be seen from the driver's position.

The back of the bus, of course, offered total privacy. But it was also a minefield of danger. At the back of the bus, you couldn't be seen by the driver, but you could be found by all the other kids who didn't want to be seen.

Our driver didn't wait for me to choose a preference.

Off we went, with me still standing in the aisle, lucky to be upright as the bus wheels labored up the dirt road. I gripped the back rests of the seats and made my way deeper into the transport. If I didn't choose quickly, I'd still be standing in the aisle, clinging to the seats when we stopped on another corner. I passed the two first open benches, then three more already filled with kids. I quickly sat down in the next row that didn't have a body in it.

Nobody made eye contact.

Just how I liked it.

I popped in some headphones and stared out the window. Judging by the number of students already seated, my stop was fairly early in the route. Fixing my bike would have to be a priority. It was going to be a long commute. Seeing the geography of the town and driving over every back road, nook, and cranny wasn't an ideal way to spend almost an hour before school. Traveling through the patchwork of town, we stopped and started on every corner, filling the bus with kids.

I stuck my backpack on the seat beside me as a gentle reminder that everyone should make an effort to find their own space before encroaching on mine, but soon I could see the passenger list was longer than a single-space occupancy would allow. I dodged the first couple bullets as kids recognized their friends and quickly sat with them, but my luck couldn't hold out forever. When the seat across the aisle from me filled to double capacity, I knew it was only a matter of time.

The girl who became my seatmate didn't ask to sit so much as she stopped and raised an eyebrow in my general direction.

I wordlessly obliged by picking up my bag and plopping it on my lap.

She swung herself in beside me, careful not to touch me. We rode the rest of the way in total silence, each doing our best not to disturb the other, a sheet of her straight, shoulder-length black hair dividing our bus bench in half.

She was the perfect seatmate.

It was a trip of total anonymity.

Once she had settled, the girl grabbed an anime graphic novel from her backpack and wordlessly flipped through it. We lived in excellent, mutual silence.

But with the kid in the row in front of me, I wasn't so lucky.

"You're new."

The freckled girl twisted around in her seat and sat on her own bent knee to elevate and see me better. She and my seatmate ignored each other so completely that I knew they knew each other well.

"Just moved in," I agreed, offering a forced smile to prove I meant no aggression.

"No, I've seen you before."

"I have a bike?" I suggested.

Maybe she'd seen me riding through town.

"Then what are you doing here on the bus?"

"Good point." I chuckled, but she wasn't being rhetorical. "Oh, it has a flat tire."

"I had a flat tire once. My bike's only a five speed. We got it from Turk's Used Bike Shop in the next town over. You know, Alderton? It's a pretty nice store, but not enough ten speeds. At a store like that, there only is what there is. Know what I mean?"

She didn't wait for an answer.

"I like the bus." She shrugged. "You get to meet people."

I felt the girl beside me stifle a laugh.

"Maybe we'll have a class together. I'm Kate Hucklebee. And that's Josie Jew." She nodded at my seatmate.

"Jiu," the quiet girl corrected without looking up from her book.

"That's what I said."

Kate rolled her eyes. *Some people could be so picky,* her look seemed to say.

"A class together would be great," Kate affirmed again.

"Maybe," I agreed.

I didn't tell her, but I was kind of with my seatmate. Wanting others to use the correct pronunciation of one's name seemed totally reasonable to me.

Just then, the driver applied the brake and made a sharp right turn into the parking lot.

Our bodies lurched with the bus, but it didn't rattle Kate.

"Ooh, or we could have lockers near each other," she said.

Something told me that would not be a great thing.

I didn't answer, but Kate hardly noticed.

"We're here!" she squealed, turning in her seat, preparing to depart.

"So we are," I agreed.

My seatmate tucked her graphic novel back into her bag.

I looked out the window at the school grounds. They were now spattered with kids greeting their long-lost school chums, their real friends, and the ones they hadn't bothered to see or speak with in the past two months of summer break. The property didn't look quite so sad with the students laughing and milling about.

Maybe I would like it here after all.

If my mom could be happy here, so could I, I thought.

Although I realized I had no idea whether she was happy or not.

Aunt Abeline had said to try and make friends.

Kate had already disembarked, but maybe I should say something to the girl who'd sat beside me. Her ride in almost silence told me that we'd get along much better than I would with a chatterbox like Kate.

Maybe she could help me find my first class?

I turned away from the window, prepared to speak, still unsure what I'd say, but she was already gone.

FIVE

TWO TRUTHS AND A LIE

"THE NEXT ACTIVITY is called two truths and a lie. How many of you have played this one before?" the teacher said, informally polling us.

Several hands went up.

Mr. Hanks nodded. "That's what I thought. Not much explanation needed then. For those of you who don't know, the game is just how it sounds. You tell your partner three things: two of them are true, honest, and one is a lie. Your partner has to guess which one is false. Okay?" he asked in that purely rhetorical, teacherly way.

When no one answered, he clapped his hands together.

"Time to get to know your fellow classmates."

He pointed at an unsuspecting girl. Although it had been only minutes since he'd taken attendance, it was clear our names had already escaped him.

"You are?"

"Tharjiha."

"Okay, Tharjiha and Kinsey. Jesse and…?"

"Anne," the next girl answered.

Mr. Hanks nodded along.

"Jesse and Anne. Tyrone and Heidi, yes, you two. Red shirt and blue shirt…"

He directed traffic.

I waited for my turn in the student roundup.

In this second class of the day, there were two familiar faces: the boy from the parking lot from a couple days ago and Kate from the bus. I kind of hoped I wouldn't get partnered with either one.

"I'll partner with Marcy," a boy in a polo shirt offered.

I looked over.

The girl whom I guessed was Marcy was already getting a shoulder rub from his hands.

"No thanks, Greg. You obviously already know Ms. Galvas pretty well. You go with Katherine. Marcy, meet Gwen."

The couple frowned as the teacher went on pairing kids with new classmates.

Mr. Hanks pointed at me next.

"Mae," I offered.

"Mae, meet Peter."

My eyes flickered to the boy from the parking lot, but he didn't flinch.

Not Peter.

I blushed.

Okay, so maybe I wanted to partner with him a

little.

Quickly, I nodded at the actual Peter, who gave me a half-hearted wave, before anyone could notice my eyeline had gone askance.

"Spade and the other Peter, Peter Clatt," the teacher continued to call.

This time, parking lot guy did acknowledge the teacher's commandment.

I wish I could say that I was minding my own business, but I just couldn't help myself. I quickly learned, his name was Peter Clatt... or Spade.

My Peter partner grinned and pushed his buddy towards my parking lot friend.

"Have fun, Pete," he joked.

The other Peter rolled his eyes.

I pretended I wasn't keenly watching. But of course, I took every detail in.

So, drive-by's name was Spade.

Typical hot guy name.

I rolled my eyes to myself and purposefully turned my back to him. It would be good to meet some new people, starting with my new partner.

Peter.

He made his way over to me.

"Hey," I opened.

"New here, huh?" he asked. He was still grinning at his friend, who was swatting his hand behind his back as though he could feel both our eyes and our teasing judgment upon him.

"Yeah, my aunt and I just moved."

"Is Plumpkin everything you ever dreamed?"

"Actually, I didn't even know we were coming. She sort of sprang it on me last minute. That's kind of how she rolls. You've been here…"

"All my life. Small town living."

"Ms. Kingsley and Mr. Stine, two truths and one lie," the teacher reminded us.

We were actually having a real conversation and legitimately learning more about each other, so of course we should break that up and use his artificial framework to pretend to get to know each other instead.

I could already tell Peter was cool.

"I'm six feet tall, I'm allergic to marshmallows, and Pete's my half brother," he offered.

I sized him up.

He could definitely be six feet tall, it would be hard to know his allergies without provoking a reaction, and there was no way the Peters were brothers. They got along too well.

"Truth, truth, lie."

"Hah! I actually messed it up. I'm six feet one and marshmallows make me blow up like the Fourth of July. So that was two lies." He puffed out his cheeks and exploded them like a firecracker bursting in air. "But you were right. Pete's not my brother. How did you know?"

"I doubt a parent would be sick enough to name both their kids the exact same thing… and a lot of couples look alike." I shrugged.

Peter grinned. "Is it that obvious?"

"Yes," Greg said, butting in.

Turns out his partner, Katherine, was Kate from the bus, and he was about as interested in spending time with her as I was.

"Peter and Peter are boyfriend and boyfriend," Kate added, coming behind Greg, two steps too late.

"Thank you for announcing my romantic status," Peter loudly criticized.

He rolled his eyes and turned us away. Greg was on his own with Katherine.

"What's yours?" Peter asked.

"Oh, I don't have a boyfriend."

"Your two truths and a lie."

"Right... I hate these games," I admitted.

"You don't think they help us become lifelong friends?"

"Oh, we're lifelong friends." I laughed. "You're too charming not to be."

Peter cracked a smile too.

I'd won him over.

"Can I come hang with you guys? My partner's too cool for me," the other Peter whimpered, tucking his body in beside us so Mr. Hanks wouldn't see.

"That's okay, I think the teacher's wrapping up anyway," I agreed, ready to give them space.

"Maybe next round you should go with Spade," the other Peter suggested.

"No, I'm good, I—"

"You said you don't have a boyfriend…" my Peter noted.

"Oh! Spade's available," the other Peter said.

"He's always available." My Peter chuckled.

"Not interested." I shook my head.

"That was a quick denial."

"Real quick." The other Peter smiled.

"I'm not denying, I'm just not interested."

"Hmm."

The boys grinned at each other, happy to tease me.

"The lady doth protest too much…" my Peter hinted.

"I think there's a bit of interest." His boyfriend agreed.

"Well, who wouldn't be?"

As the guys swooped in more and more, I rolled my eyes, suddenly in need of some air.

"Switch," Mr. Hanks called out.

The Peters gave me a little push in Spade's direction.

I looked up too late and almost bumped into him.

"Oh, sorry."

I quickly turned, and instead, bumped into another student.

"Sorry." I apologized to them too.

That kid frowned and quickly pushed their way to partner with someone else.

Helpless, I turned again, but everyone had settled with their new conversationalists.

Everyone but Spade.

He was waiting for me.

Peter and Peter both grinned and gave me a little wave.

I did my best to ignore them, but there was nowhere else to go. Even Kate was already on a roll with another partner who looked less than thrilled to be there. I turned back to my parking lot friend, knowing he was waiting.

"Flat tire." He grinned at me by way of introduction.

"Your name is Spade?"

He shrugged. "My mom was a hippie... Spade's actually my last name... and I think I'm in love with you."

"Truth, truth, and a lie."

He smiled.

I frowned, trying to think of my own witty scenario. Something about this guy made me feel like I had to be on my toes.

"I'm new in town..."

"Truth."

"I don't know anybody..."

"Truth."

"And my hair's on fire."

"You're kind of an odd bird, you know that?"

"I've been called worse. Just finish the game."

"Truth, truth, and a lie."

"You got me," I said, sarcasm dripping from my voice.

"Do I?" Spade asked, a delicious smile on his lips.

My cheeks flushed crimson.

"No, I..."

"Okay everyone, back to your seats," Mr. Hanks called us back to attention.

Spade gave me a wink and ambled back to his desk on the other side of the room.

"Hey, hi!"

In the class shifting, Kate made her way beside me, her favorite busmate.

"I didn't know you were into computer art."

That's because you don't know anything about me, I thought to myself. But I forced a smile on my face. Kate was genuinely pleased to see me, and I felt a twinge of guilt. Here she was, being totally welcoming, and even if it was only in my mind, I was treating her like a jerk.

"It was the only elective that fit into my schedule," I confessed. "I don't even have the prerequisite. I had to get special permission."

"Well, don't worry. I can show you the ropes."

"Thanks..." I said, and I meant it. "Do you know everybody here?"

"Kinda. It's a small town. Most of the kids have been here year after year."

"What's that guy's name?"

Afraid to point, I nodded vaguely in Spade's direction.

"Spade Polari? Or Kendal Base?"

"Never mind." I shrugged.

"Weren't you just partnered with him? He was supposed to introduce himself."

"Yeah, weird." I sat back in my chair, trying to appear nonchalant.

I should have stopped while I was ahead, but I just couldn't help myself.

"Are you sure Spade's not his last name?"

"Pretty sure. Why?"

"I guess he was just messing with me."

"Sounds like that was definitely his lie. It's a dumb icebreaker." She shrugged.

"Yeah. Silly."

"Okay. Listen up! This time, it's new partners and a new discussion. Would you rather! A tough choice between two equally awful options. Pick your poison with your partner and discuss... Find a new classmate. Would you rather eat a plate full of hot peppers on a first date or have a frozen mouth full of Novocaine on prom night. Switch it up!"

Mr. Hanks reordered the class.

This time I was partnered with a quiet girl named Gwen.

We dutifully answered the question, but I didn't really hear anything she was saying. I just kept asking myself the same question: if his quip about his last name was Spade's lie, what was his truth?

SIX

THE MISSING MOON

"THERE SHE IS, our little school girl. Tell me all about it," Aunt Abeline cooed as I walked in the door. She was playing with the letters on her Scrabble rack, no doubt about to murder me with another seventy-point word.

"What?"

"Your first day."

"It's not my first day ever." I rolled my eyes. "I've been to plenty of schools before."

"I know. But it was your first day here."

"It was fine."

I plopped my empty backpack on my flip-flops and tried to blow past. I didn't really need the canvas bag yet, but we'd likely receive all our textbooks by the end of the week. So far, I only had one and I'd left it in my locker.

"Not so fast, sullen teenager."

"That wasn't sullen!"

I laughed, but I still didn't want to divulge anything real. I hadn't one hundred percent forgiven her for dangling my dead mom's memory like a carrot.

"It was fine. No biggie. Same as always. What's in the oven?"

"Spinach casserole."

"Oh."

Involuntarily, I scrunched my nose.

"I saw that. It's good for you. Good for those bones." She laughed, looking me over.

But suddenly, her face blanched ghostly white.

"Where's your necklace?"

In reply, my hand naturally floated up to my collarbone, but quickly I realized she wasn't talking about my neck. She was looking for my grandmother's moon charm. The one I'd worn as an anklet. I looked down at my foot but felt the truth before I saw for myself.

"Oh..."

The jewelry was gone. Oh crap. When did that happen?

"My new friend at school, Kate," I said, quick on my feet, "liked it so much she asked if she could borrow it." I peeked at my aunt's face. It wasn't clear if she was buying it. "But I just realized I should have brought my textbook home. Do you think you could take me back so I can grab it? I'd hate to skip the homework on my very first day."

"You let her borrow it?" Aunt Abeline looked concerned.

"Uh-huh. For a date. You said to make friends. Will you take me back?"

"I guess I did," she agreed. "Just let me get my purse."

The second she left the room I picked up my backpack and checked my shoes, but the chain wasn't dropped among the sandal thongs.

"I'll meet you at the car!" I called.

I flew outdoors, searching the gravel walkway. The rustic terrain could hide a lot of things at first glance, but I had to act fast. I wanted to find the family trinket before Aunt Abeline knew it was gone. Luckily, the shiny gold would stick out in the tiny rocks.

It wasn't there either.

"We'll make this quick," she said as she came outside. "The casserole's in the oven."

"I'll be like two secs," I agreed.

My aunt drove the speed limit, but it felt like we were crawling. Every extra second that we took could be another moment someone else could find and take the little moon. I willed the car to move faster. Before today, my aunt had never said anything about me wearing the necklace either around my neck or as an anklet, but that didn't mean I could be careless. It was a family antique. I should have known better.

"I'm sorry about the anklet, Aunt Abby. I didn't know I shouldn't share it—"

"Oh, honey. I know." She patted my knee, her expression softening. "As long as it's returned, that's what counts."

There was a strange tone in her voice... or was I imagining it?

The schoolyard was empty. The first day of school was officially over, although there were still a few cars left in the parking lot.

"I'll be super quick." I practically jumped out while the vehicle was still rolling, but I wanted to be sure Aunt Abeline stayed in the car.

I hurried up to the same double doors that the other day had denied my entrance, pulled the door open, and slipped inside.

I felt terrible about losing the anklet. I'd worn it twenty or thirty times before and never felt even a little slip on my foot. Today, I had been so preoccupied with being the new kid, I didn't feel it when it disappeared.

And now, even worse, I was lying to my aunt.

The whole point of being responsible was to get her to trust me so I could learn more about our family, but here I was, sneaking around, covering up my lapse in judgment. The irony wasn't lost on me.

Looking closely at the linoleum tiles, I saw a disgusting amount of hair and dust bunnies, gum wrappers, bottle caps, even two quarters, but no sign of my missing charm or a necklace. Eventually, I'd covered all the ground I traversed that day and circled back to the front of the school. No luck.

There was nothing more to do tonight.

I doubled back to my locker and grabbed the textbook. If I was going to tell a lie, at least I'd be thorough.

"Did you find what you were looking for?" Aunt Abeline asked as I popped back in the car.

"Right here." I waved the book in my lap. I couldn't bring myself to make eye contact.

"Then let's go."

She tilted the gearshift and kicked the car into drive.

I stared out the window. Where might it have gone? In one of the classrooms? After school they were locked. In the morning, I'd check first thing. We rode for a while in silence.

"Be sure to get the moon back." She nodded as we rolled back into the driveway. "It was important to your mother."

I felt too racked with guilt to even ask what she meant.

"It'll be back before you know it," I agreed.

SEVEN

A DIP IN THE MOONLIGHT

THE STRESS of the first day at a new school, or maybe the loss of my grandma's necklace, or possibly even the crispy, overcooked spinach casserole we ended up eating for dinner kept me up well into the night. I lay in bed, listening to the hum of the mouse prevention buzzer singing its high-pitched, unpleasant song.

Even with pillows stuffed over my ears, I could not stifle the hum.

I weighed my options.

If I kept the buzzer plugged in, my room would remain rodent-free, but I'd likely never sleep again. If I disconnected the little hummer, I might finally get some rest, but I could wake at any moment to a room infested with four-legged friends. The best choice, I decided, was to split the difference. I would unplug the buzzer at bedtime, but reconnect the deterrent at the start of each morning. While I was at school, the little white box could work its whiny magic. At night, I'd sleep in silent peace. That seemed the best of both worlds. Hopefully, those unpleasant days would be enough to keep my nights free of rodents.

I opened the covers, dragged myself out of bed, and pulled the plug out of the wall. Immediately, the room filled with silence.

Much better.

It was so quiet here. Now that we were out of the city, I was getting used to the hush.

I could hear the wind in the trees much more clearly. Humans and their smorgasbords of machinery created their own sort of buzz, just like the mouse trap, but here in Plumpkin, that general din disappeared. It was so still.

I crashed back onto my bed.

Was it possible that the silence was also deafening?

I closed my eyes and tried to imagine a gentle setting sun lowering into a peaceful, somber evening. The night sky would fill with stars, and peace and love would settle on the world. If I could picture it, maybe I'd lull my body into slumber. But no visualization worked. I was wide awake.

I sighed and plugged the mouse deterrent buzzer back into the wall.

If I wasn't going to sleep, I may as well keep the space free of vermin.

Suddenly, outside, a wash of blue light fell on the windowsill.

The moon had come out.

The whole day and evening had been sort of gloomy and overcast, so the moon had been hidden and lackluster under the cover of clouds. But now, in the middle of the night, the storm had passed and the sky had cleared. The moon returned to its nighttime glory. It was amazing how bright the reflection was. All the shapes in my room took on a luminous glow.

I loved a full moon. Who didn't?

I went to the window and peeked out the curtain. The forest glistened with a blue-and-silver color palette coating every twig and branch. The trees were eerily, beautifully visible. I felt a childlike impulse to run my hands on their bark.

Why not? I wasn't sleeping.

I pulled on my terry cloth robe and headed down to the lake. In the bright, clear night sky, I didn't need a flashlight to guide the way. I could easily see my route.

What a whirlwind first day, I thought, picking my way down to the lake.

The Peters seemed nice, and Kate was... Kate. My science teacher seemed kind of strict, but that was okay. You wanted a little strictness in the compulsory credits. Maybe this year I'd try out for field hockey, and... oh, who was I kidding? My brain ping-ponged over and over back to two important topics. My missing moon necklace and the cute boy named Spade.

What kind of name was Spade anyway?

Not a last name, that was for sure.

I was surprised to learn the boy from the parking

lot had taken up so much real estate in my brain. I barely knew him.

I picked up a smooth rock and skipped it across the lake surface.

It bounced one, two, three times before dipping below the water's edge.

I stared up into the heavens. This was a beautiful place on earth. Here, from the lakeside, the sky was enormous. The clouds had fully dispersed, leaving the atmosphere open, full of starlight. I looked up at the teeny-tiny planets, the stars, and even the distant galaxies reflecting their light back to me.

The world was so big, and I was just this tiny speck of existence.

In this milky, bright night, my anklet moon charm would have fit in perfectly.

Maybe Spade had found it, and all would be right with the world.

As the thought popped into my head, it actually brought a lot of comfort.

If Spade did find my necklace, I felt confident that I would get it back.

I stuck my big toe in the lapping water. The lake was still warm from the heat of summer. The autumn nights had yet to bring their chilly edge. There weren't too many days of swimming left. I looked around at the other cottages. I was the only person by the water. This was to be expected for a midnight visit, but a lot of the owners' absences from the lakeshore were more permanent than that. Most of the buildings were already locked down for the winter season, their humans long gone to sturdier homes until next spring's annual pilgrimage began. Those who were still here were safely sleeping in their beds. Their doors and windows were locked and dark for the night.

It was such a pity to waste such a beautiful evening.

I stepped farther into the bay, up to my feet at first, then to my ankles. The water felt wonderful.

A nighttime dip would help me relax, I realized.

It seemed so inviting.

I could run up to the cabin and change into my swimsuit... but I shouldn't wake Aunt Abeline. She didn't know I was out here. I looked back to our house. It was pitch black. I hadn't turned on a single light when I left. I wouldn't want to disturb her. Maybe I should call it a night.

Or... a little voice inside me countered.

You could go for a skinny dip.

Where did that thought come from?

I grinned to myself.

Did I dare?

Who would it harm?

I looked around again, but only confirmed what I already knew. There wasn't a soul on the lake. Suddenly, my heart raced in my chest. I was seriously considering it.

Why not?

Uh, because Aunt Abeline would kill me?!

But what she didn't know wouldn't hurt her. My

missing necklace was a prime example of that. I peered back over my shoulder at the blackened cottage windows. There she was, sleeping soundly. A little dalliance on my part would go by totally unnoticed.

What the hell!

I slipped off my robe and folded it neatly on the dock chair.

The cool air kissed my skin. I couldn't help but giggle. It already felt so illicit standing there in just a tank top and undies, with the wind grazing over my bare arms and legs.

Maybe it was the knowledge that I'd decided to break a rule.

Maybe it was the act of moving out of my comfort zone.

Either way, it felt exhilarating, and like something I would never attempt if I weren't alone.

I moved the chair off the deck and sunk its feet into the sandy shore beside the water. Once settled, I still felt unsatisfied and relocated the chair maybe six or seven inches again. The final move was totally unnecessary, but I felt a little internal nudge that everything had to be perfect if I was going to proceed.

The breeze tickled my bare body.

I felt my arm hair goose pimple in anticipation.

Skinny-dipping was the kind of brave, silly thing independent girls did in the movies. In real life, it felt like I was exposing myself to a reckless, unnecessary risk... and it turned out that was exhilarating.

I snuck one final look around and, certain I was

alone, I stripped off my tank top and undies. I chucked them in the direction of the neatly folded robe and strove into the liquid cover of night. The *whoosh* of the water around me set my skin a-tingle.

A rush of excitement.

The coolness kissed every part of my bones.

My breasts felt free and buoyant. The water was cold but not unpleasant. It refreshed every inch of my skin. It was amazing to discover how much those little squares of fabric covering our most private parts could reign us in. Tonight, I savored being free in the water's embrace. I ducked my head underwater, pushed off the sandy bottom, and swam deeper into the lake.

Eek!

A piece of seaweed touched my leg.

I involuntarily shuddered and wiggled out of its floating grasp. The lake was a living, breathing thing already teeming with underwater life. I briefly worried about tiny minnows getting confused and swimming up my urethra, but my irrational fears couldn't outweigh the freedom and joy I felt at being wildly free and one with nature in a way I'd never been before. Already, the early rush of cool water against my skin had acclimatized into a refreshing cleanse. I cut through the water in a front crawl. Keeping my splashing to a minimum, I felt graceful and fast. I swam out farther into the lake, well beyond the waters that might be considered part of our property, then folded back the way I'd come, diving under and resurfacing once more.

Seeking some sort of destination, I made my way to a floating milk jug two properties over that marked a large tree stump poking up from deep waters. Its existence warned the dangerous presence of underwater debris to the local boat drivers, but also made for a perfect swimming goal.

I arrived at it quickly.

There was little current to stop me.

I circled the buoy and redirected my journey, making my way back home. I swam that same route three or four times, just for the thrill of it. When I'd expended most of my nervous energy, my body relaxed, and I settled into the waters at home.

I grew braver too.

I lay out on my back, my arms and legs floating by my sides with three bright white bumps in my midsection. My two breasts and the curve of my tummy broke the water's surface. They were followed by my thighs and finally my toes.

I sank my ears into the water and stared up to the heavens. I felt one with the universe. It was so big and vast, and I was so tiny and small, but we belonged together, part of the same life force, part of the same indescribable heaven.

I thought about all the kids stuck in cities. They would never get to appreciate such a miraculous night sky, or the gift of experiencing nature so totally alone.

Perhaps coming to stay in Plumpkin long-term was actually a good thing.

Maybe it was the best thing to ever happen to me?

Or maybe my mind was full of adrenaline and dopamine.

The cool water had released so many endorphins.

I was relaxed and happy to my very core.

It was time for bed.

I treaded water, moving slowly towards the shoreline, towards my discarded clothing, when suddenly, to my left, I heard a tree branch snap.

What was that?

I whipped my head in that direction, all my senses returning to high alert.

There it was again.

Suddenly, I was hyperaware.

Snap, snap.

Something was moving through the forest. Coming quickly.

My breath labored heavy in my throat.

Crack, crack.

With one little sound, everything had become different.

I was still naked in the lake.

But I was no longer alone.

EIGHT

DISGRACE IN BACK-TO-BACK GENERATIONS

MY EYES SEARCHED THE DARKNESS. I sank low, my head barely above the water. The moon beams highlighted every crooked branch, every scrubby brush. Was someone in the woods? I held very still and listened.

Crack, crack.

There was the movement, again.

It was hard to hear the sounds of the forest over the rush of blood pumping in my ears, but it was there.

I was certain of it.

My head panned from the trees to my clothes strewn on the shore. They were all still there, robe on the chair, tank and undies hanging off, exactly where I'd thrown them. Nothing had moved.

Then, something did.

I almost laughed out loud.

A squirrel, or a chipmunk... maybe an otter? I wasn't really sure.

Some small woodland creature scurried out of the thicket, scampered across the beach, and thrust itself deep into the forest. Like a little bolt of lightning, it shot across the forest floor.

Crack, crack.

It bent more twigs on its exit trajectory, but it was over as quickly as it had come.

I was alone with my thoughts once more.

Just to be sure, I held still longer than I'd ever thought possible, but that was the only sound. The forest was quiet.

Because I wasn't moving my body, or perhaps because when my fight-or-flight response kicked in all the blood had drained out of the extraneous veins in my body, it had grown chilly in the water. I was cold. It was definitely time to get out.

Getting into the lake naked had been freeing and exhilarating, but getting out wasn't nearly as fun. Even though my brain knew the sounds in the woods hadn't come from a human, I couldn't shake my disgruntled nerves.

I worried that someone was watching.

Instead of free and careless, I felt open and exposed once more.

I hurried out of the water, wrapping the robe around my cold, damp, naked body. My wet skin soaked the fabric. It clung to me in all the wrong places, but the material also felt safe and warm. I cursed the fact that I hadn't thought to bring a towel. I grabbed my underwear from the ground and ungracefully stepped into the leg holes. I yanked them up my body. They caught on wet skin patches and tugged and stretched too far, but as soon I had on those little squares of fabric, my dignity was protected once more.

I felt a little better.

I shoved my tank top into the pocket of my robe, tugged the opening of the housecoat closer at the neck for both warmth and safety, and headed back up the path towards our cabin. My flip-flops rubbed raw against my wet feet now mixed with rough sand. I didn't bother to fix them. Now that I was cold, I didn't want to spend any extra time exposed to the elements, so I did my best to ignore the discomfort my feet presented and traveled on tiptoe back to the house.

Quickly up the path, I was about to open the screened porch door, but I stopped with my hand on the handle.

Aunt Abeline was pacing inside.

I froze.

Was she looking for me? Was she angry?

We'd never discussed what I could and couldn't do in the middle of the night. Obviously, the desired place for a teenage girl after midnight would be at home, safe in bed. But I couldn't sleep, and the lake had seemed like a jaunty fix.

Was that so wrong?

Instinctively, I knew she would disapprove of my naked night swimming, even if it was just me and an otter or two, but I didn't think my small act of defiance would have her up out of bed.

It was strange though.

She hadn't turned on any overhead lights. Just one small lamp.

And there was something off-putting about the look on her face.

Even in the shadows, I could tell by the crook of her arm that she was on the phone, and she was pacing, something she only did when she was worried or receiving bad news.

No, on second thought, this wasn't about me or my night swimming.

She didn't know I was awake, or why would she stay huddled in the near dark?

I took my hand off the doorknob and slinked back into the shadows to observe her, wiping my wet, matted hair off my face.

"That's what she said," she said. "Well, I know."

The other person in the conversation seemed to go on and on.

"He better find it tomorrow. Uh-huh."

Aunt Abeline was listening hard, worked up over what the other person was saying. But after a moment, she softened, even chuckled. The other person seemed to have calmed her fears.

"Well, we can't be disgraced in back-to-back generations... I know. It worked well for Sierra; it should work for her too... I will... Okay. Talk soon, with better news... okay... bye-bye." Aunt Abeline placed her device on the table.

Worked well for Sierra?

Disgrace in back-to-back generations?

I took in the tiny snippets of conversation.

Who on earth was my aunt talking to at two or three in the morning? And why did she bring up Mom's name? I had so many questions.

I willed my aunt to pick up the phone and say something, anything more.

This was very strange.

A third mention of my mother in as many days was wildly out of character.

Sierra Kingsley.

My dearly departed mother.

I was grateful to Aunt Abeline for taking me in, raising me, and sharing her many homes with me after my mom passed away. But for us that name was a lightning rod. We never spoke about Sierra. We never spoke about anything of consequence. Not our family history, not distant relatives. For that part of my life, I was starved for specifics. Everyone but us was dead and gone. But Aunt Abeline was sure I was too young to know the details. For her to mention my mother, even in passing on a late-night phone call, felt really important. But much as I begged the night sky for further information, the conversation was over.

I wasn't going to glean any more.

I had a weird feeling my aunt was discussing my missing anklet. Did she know it was lost? She seemed to buy into my friendship story. Although if imaginary Kate never brought the necklace back, she'd catch on quickly. I couldn't exactly replace it. If it disappeared and I couldn't find it, the charm would be gone for good. Did my aunt already suspect this?

No, that was silly. I was reading too much into it.

I waited in the cold for as long as I could manage, asking myself more and more strange questions that I knew I could never answer, running her half of the conversation over in my head.

What "worked" for my mom?

How could I possibly disgrace another generation?

And with whom, at three a.m. on a Tuesday, was she talking over these details?

Still, I held fast where I was.

I didn't want to start that conversation or any other with my aunt from my current position, soaking and cold. If I asked her face-to-face what this was all about, I didn't want to give her any easy distractions on which to hang my disgrace. If she was willing to discuss the details with a stranger in a phone call in the middle of the night, in secret, it was clear this was something she didn't want me to know.

No, if I was going to get any answers, I would need to come from a position of power that a sopping wet robe and ratty hair would not net. I couldn't let her see me like this, so I waited.

Aunt Abeline disappeared into the depths of the house.

After about twenty minutes of air-drying, I decided I had waited long enough. She had probably gone to sleep, and I was longing for a warm, comfortable bed myself.

It was time to take my chance.

I slipped open the screen door with barely a hinge squeak and slipped off my shoes at the door. I inched into the kitchen on high alert for any movement, but was relieved to hear the quiet, rhythmic snores of my aunt down the hall. She was asleep in her bed. I padded my way down the hallway and dipped back into my own bedroom, careful not to let the door closing behind me make so much as a click. Without turning on a light for guidance, I stripped off the wet robe and undergarments, patted my clammy skin with a hand towel, and slipped on a fresh nightshirt and clean pair of undies from the dresser.

The sheets felt like a warm, comforting hug as I climbed back into bed.

I pulled the soft, dry fabric under my chin and vowed to get answers to all the questions in the morning. Even with the mouse deterrent buzzer humming in the corner, I fell asleep almost immediately.

NINE

THE MOON HAS DECIDED

IN MY DREAMS, I found myself back outside, dressed in a billowy black dress with layers of crinoline floating around my legs. I walked up to a stone staircase. Higher and higher I climbed, the stiff fabric of my dress scratching my legs, my bare feet cold on the cement slabs. The moon hung low and bright in the sky, casting its blue-gray hue on everything around me. Eventually, the stones gave way to a wooden boardwalk, and I walked down the planks through the mist to reach the water's edge.

There, waiting with its bow dipped low in the water, was an old green canoe.

In dreamland, I didn't have to pick up the layers and layers of dress, or delicately balance, or crawl to my seat in the boat. I simply climbed aboard and found myself safely ensconced in its gunnels. The gauze of my dress created a cupcake of fabric to sit on. I floated away from the shore and began to paddle, sitting high on one of the two seats in the small boat. I dipped the oar low in the water, and when it resurfaced it was no longer a wooden paddle; it had changed from an oar into a snake.

Hiss.

Its forked tongue flickered in my face. Instinctively, I threw it out in front of me. The snake clanked off the gutter and recoiled in the bottom of the boat, hissing as it regathered. I looked at the empty seat in the front of the boat for help. But there was no one there. The snake recoiled, getting ready to strike. Its face rose up before me and soon, all around me in the water, more snakes slithered towards my path.

Frantic, I stood up on my seat.

The boat rocked dangerously as my center of gravity rose, and I stepped behind the small latticework bench that had held my weight moments ago. There was nowhere to go. I was already positioned at the back of the boat.

With all my weight so uneven in the vessel, the canoe started to tip, its bow rising above the water into the air.

Desperate, I looked back down at the latticework seat I'd been sitting on.

Suddenly, it was no longer a chair, but a pathway I could see right through. I leaned forward farther and looked deeper.

The latticework weave of the bench grew larger, morphing into prison bars.

But I was on the outside looking in.

Inside was the girl from the bus. She turned and looked right at me, sad and resolute.

"The moon has decided," she said.

"Decided what?" I asked, but it was too late.

Her eyes rolled back in her head and her jaw unhinged, opening, creating a tunnel for the roller coaster I now sat in to dive through, plunging me and everyone else in the chain of cars into total darkness. I hung on for dear life. The car flung left and right. We shot directly towards a statue with raised, outstretched arms. As the rattling car drew closer, the appendages burst into a flock of black crows. They swooped out towards me.

I ducked my head in terror, but the murder flew in a cluster and soared past overhead.

Abruptly, we pulled up to a stop.

The safety protection bar over my dress let up. We were now free to get out.

I was about to stand when something at the bottom of the coaster car caught my eye.

It was an orange-and-white tabby cat.

The pet meowed and flopped over, asking for a belly rub.

I petted his soft, squirmy tummy and when I looked up, the rest of the passengers were departing the cars. I stood, along with the girl from the bus. We moved to exit the car. Somehow in dream logic she was both a passenger and the architect and structure of the ride itself.

I tried to follow her route to the side exit, but she walked out on a tightrope.

She took one small step and then another.

She balanced on the line, her agile feet moving quickly.

But several steps in, her eyes widened in terror.

She teetered.

Her weight fluctuated forward and to compensate, she lunged her hips back. There was too much momentum. She reached out for me, but before my fingers could grasp her, she slipped off the line and fell.

Her bloodcurdling scream pierced my conscious mind.

I sat straight up in bed.

My hair was matted and weird from going to sleep with a wet head, and I'd never been so happy to see the morning light.

TEN

THE DEATH CERTIFICATE

"DID I hear you last night? Were you talking to someone?" I asked my aunt casually as I put my breakfast into the toaster.

As was our regular routine, Aunt Abeline had come out of her bedroom before me in the morning and she was drinking her usual coffee in her favorite oversized mug. Since I'd awoken so early this morning, I'd come to realize that my little walk on the wet-and-wild side of life last night had made me a bit overdramatic. That late-night phone call Aunt Abeline took was just some weird but normal part of life. My aunt would explain it all away. I just had to ask her about it and play it cool. Get my answers without tipping my hand that I was up half the night, swimming naked in the lake.

"Oh, pish. Was I talking in my sleep? I did have some outrageous dreams. Did I say anything dippy?"

I felt my whole body sink.

I was wrong.

She was playing dumb.

Aunt Abeline was up to something, and she had no intention of telling me what was going on.

"I think it was something about Mom or Grandma Mim," I tried again. "Something generational."

"Generational... huh. That's a big word." Aunt Abeline took a long sip of coffee. "I should play that on the board... if it wasn't longer than seven letters..." She let her thoughts drift away, fumbling with her tray of Scrabble letters.

The toast in the toaster popped for its second time. I pulled the hot bread from the elements.

"Oh, I know what it was. I was in a cake-eating contest in my dream, can you imagine? And your grandma's recipe came in third place. That woman could bake a heavenly dessert. Her best was strawberry rhubarb, although I think in the dream, it might have been chocolate. Funny that you heard. Did you catch any details?"

"Ouch!"

The just cooked bread burned my fingertips.

Protectively, I popped the pink tips into my mouth to suck on the pain and give myself a moment to think. My mind reeled.

Now she was trolling for answers?

She was testing to learn what I had heard?

"Are you okay?" Aunt Abeline started to get up to come to my aid, but I stepped backwards. "You have to be careful."

Suddenly, I didn't want her anywhere near me.

"I gotta catch the bus," I said.

I left the hot toast on the counter and grabbed my school bag. I avoided the sandy flip-flops from the night before and shoved my feet into a pair of sneakers instead.

"But your breakfast…"

"I'm not hungry," I called over my shoulder, already on my way out the door. I could feel the panic rising in front of me.

Why was she lying?

"Don't forget to retrieve that necklace," she called to my back.

That only confirmed what I thought.

That late-night phone call *was* about me.

It was definitely about my mom. It might have been about my necklace?

Okay, yeah, I'd done a dumb thing, losing a family heirloom, then I'd done a second stupid thing, going for a naked dip in the lake, but there was a difference between us. If she'd asked about either of those things, I would have confessed. I'd have confessed them both! She might have thought less of me, been a little disappointed, but to undertake a secret chat in the middle of the night?

She was having clandestine phone calls, talking to someone about me and my mother, building up some generational shame between us, and when I asked her about it, she lied to my face.

I walked to the bus stop in a blind mix of fear,

confusion, and rage. I felt betrayed. Your closest family members weren't supposed to lie and manipulate. What else was she hiding? I was so sick and tired of the secrets. If you don't want to talk, fine, you don't want to talk. But don't keep bringing her up. The most secretive topic in my life. The only thing we constantly pretended to ignore. She was my life's biggest question.

Sierra.

A mystery illness took her without warning.

Mom died and we all just moved on. Never to be spoken of again.

The way I remembered it, one day everything was fine. We were doing usual mother-daughter things like eating ice cream in the park, or putting cushions in blanket forts, and the next, she was in a hospital bed, tubes coming out of every orifice, machines whirring and pumping, her body immediately wilting.

I was only four.

That's when my aunt arrived.

She sat by her sister's side every day.

Sometimes I lay on the bed too. My mom was so small that she and I both fit comfortably. Other times, I played with dolls and building blocks on the floor while the sisters talked overhead.

The women looked alike.

They had distinct family markers like plump bottom lips and chiseled but slightly rounded jawbones. I had them too. They spoke for hours, and sometimes sat in total silence. But once she arrived, my aunt never really left.

Not that she had long to wait.

The doctors couldn't identify what was wrong, and since they didn't know what the matter was, nothing they did seemed to help.

Sierra's body quickly withered.

I remember thinking her bones were too sharp. They poked into my heart.

She was gone before they could even assign a diagnosis. The death certificate said "medical complications."

I kept it with me. A secret keepsake after she passed.

How many kids had their mother's death certificate in their underwear drawer?

It was the only piece of my mom that I ever really owned.

After that, I left the hospital with Aunt Abeline; I'd lived with my mother's sister ever since. She was nice to me, and strict, and social, but she never tried to take my mother's place. It was like I'd moved in with an older friend who was definitely in charge of me, but who let me discover the world on my own. She kept her silence on a lot of things. My mother. My father. Our family history. What things were like as a kid... the list went on.

I used to ask.

I used to wonder and pepper my aunt with a lot of questions, and she would try to answer, but there was always so much hurt in her eyes that before long, she or I changed the subject. She'd say, *I'll tell you when you're older.* But the less we discussed it, the older I got. It pained us both, so neither pushed the envelope more, and eventually the topics just faded away. We landed in safer planes like board games and wordplay. Aunt Abeline had a better vocabulary than anyone else I'd ever known. I was getting pretty good at wordplay too.

I think she really missed my mom. I know she loved her.

I missed and loved her too—even if I could barely remember those days.

These last few days were the most I'd heard Aunt Abeline mention Mom or Grandma Mim in years.

Ours was a quiet but happy house.

We ate together, traveled, moved around, chatted about the weather, and played the never-ending vocabulary games, but we let everything in our world float in shallow waters.

Things changed all the time.

Life was fluid.

We didn't talk about the past, her present or mine, and we rarely discussed our futures.

I didn't even know why we were constantly on the move. It was just another part of life. I would pack all my things, travel up the road to wherever life would take us, then unpack them again. We would live our daily lives for a while, make new friends, experience new things, and then, within a season or two, we would be moving again. You'd think all those unanswered questions wouldn't leave much stuff to fill the silence, but we got by just fine on pleasant, meaningless small talk and the never-ending decisions of what to eat next.

And that was our life in a nutshell...

Except for this one other thing.

There was one other mysterious piece of my mother.

A safe deposit box.

Somewhere, stored in a bank for safekeeping, there was a box in her name that was waiting for me. Promised to me. But I wasn't allowed to see it.

Not yet anyway.

Who knew what was inside?

When I was young, that box was an assurance that someone, at some time, would finally answer all of the questions I'd been collecting. My family history, my mom, the meaning of life... somehow, they'd all be stuffed inside that little bank box.

Aunt Abeline had said that one day I would open it and all those answers would be mine. But who knew when that day would arrive?

I sighed.

It was clear Aunt Abeline's secrecy today was related to my mother, and it was also true her silence on the topic was not a new experience. But that didn't make her hiding things any easier.

I think when I was young, she did it to spare my feelings, or spare herself from having to deal with my feelings. I guess she thought if we didn't speak of her sister's death or even of her memory, I'd forget that the most pivotal relationship in my life had been summarily stripped away.

One day she was there, the next she was gone.

It was so unfair. Why drudge up unanswerable questions?

But for me, it didn't work that way.

Aunt Abeline didn't seem to understand. A mother's death wasn't something you could just sweep under the carpet. It wasn't something that happened once and then was gone, never to be spoken of again. At least not when you're a kid.

Don't have a mother?

The world had a way of reminding you, again and again.

Hidden beneath our forbidden topics were gaping holes in the family history.

Land mines of pain.

Neither Aunt Abeline nor I wanted to set the other off, but sometimes I wished we could diffuse the ache.

I don't know why I thought last night's discovery would be any different.

The school bus arrived, and I pushed all the frustration to a back seat in my mind.

"Uh, hi," I said.

The driver just picked up her clipboard and checked me off her list. She swung the door closed behind me and wrestled the stick shift into drive.

"You didn't find a gold chain with a moon charm on it, did you?" I asked.

"No."

She didn't take her eyes off the road.

"Oh. Okay... thanks."

I doubted she did much of a cleaning or even a spot check at the end of her route, so I bent to look under the seats myself.

"Whatcha doin'?" Kate asked as I made my way back.

"I lost my necklace."

I peeked under the seats on either side of the aisle, but no jewelry.

"I always double clasp mine," Kate said.

How nice for you, I thought, but held my tongue.

When I was convinced the floor didn't have my chain, I got up from my hands and knees and tried to dust off the grime.

Kate made a face.

I purposefully sat down in the seat located the row behind her instead of sitting beside her and looked out the window, willing her to get the message and turn forward in her chair.

Kate was always on the bus before me, and it was common practice to plunk oneself down in the same seat as a friend so neither of you got stuck with a seatmate you didn't like, especially on a route as full as this one. So in choosing to glide past and sit by myself, I hoped to gently point out her rightful place as an acquaintance, not a friend, without being too rude.

But if she didn't take the hint soon, all pretense might disappear.

I popped in my earbuds and finally, seeing I wasn't in the mood to chat, Kate dropped back around in her seat. I exhaled the breath I didn't know I'd been holding.

After that, the bumpy route was quiet.

I stared out the dirty window and tried to silence the humming questions buzzing about in my brain.

The bus pulled up to the stop where the girl who'd sat beside me had boarded. She was there waiting for us, but at our arrival, she didn't move to get on the bus. The driver stared out at her, the bus door cranked wide open, but still the black-haired girl didn't move. Our driver waited another moment, but it was clear the girl wasn't boarding.

"Fine by me." The driver swung the door shut.

On the girl's face, I detected a bit of a smile. She hopped up off the tree stump and started walking back up the gravel road to her house.

"Wait!" I shouted.

I hurried up to the front of the bus.

"I want off. I want off the bus."

"That's not how this works." The driver clamped the bracket to lock the door. "You get on at your stop, you get off at the school."

"But I want off here."

"And I want a rich man to pay for my jet skis. Them's the breaks."

I watched helplessly as we pulled back into traffic.

"You didn't make her ride."

"Not on my bus, not my problem."

The bus lurched into the street.

I had to catch my body weight and brace for a sudden stop.

"Now go sit down," she criticized. "It's not safe to be standing."

It was pointless to draw her attention to the fact that she was the one who'd decided to drive away amidst our conversation. I weaved my way back to my empty bench.

Kate watched me arrive. Her eyes were wide as saucers.

I briefly considered avoiding her and finding a new place to sit altogether, but when I looked around for another spot to take, they were all filled.

That made sense.

The black-haired girl had only sat beside me because there were no other benches unmanned. Reluctantly, I sat back down in the row behind Kate.

"Why'd you want to get off?" she asked.

I almost laughed out loud.

Good question.

"I dunno," I admitted. "I just didn't feel like going to school."

That wasn't it, but it seemed reasonable enough. And Kate didn't push.

"Tell me about it," she agreed. "My geography teacher, Ms. Stelliston, gave us two chapters to read and sixteen questions. On the very first day! What a sadist. I have a whole after-school regime, of course, to complete all my homework. But that seems wildly excessive..." Kate continued to prattle on, leaning into my personal space, elbow dangling over my seat.

I didn't bother to try to regain my privacy.

I just punctuated her stories with enough nods and *oh yeahs* to keep her chattering the whole way to school.

Deep down, I think we both knew I didn't hear a word.

ELEVEN
LOST AND FOUND

"LET'S ask the janitor if they have anything in the lost and found," Kate suggested as we disembarked the bus.

I deeply regretted saying anything about my necklace.

Her nonstop chitchat was nearing the twenty-minute mark and what I really wanted was some quiet time to myself. I looked at the custodian raking leaves in the yard in his blue button-up shirt and navy cargo pants. The uniform made him look somehow official. He seemed almost friendly. I remembered how dirty the floors were last night. Cleaning the school was a pretty big job. Today, he was going through the motions of appearing to rake the fall leaves even though the heavy dump of autumn frost was still a few weeks away.

"I've got first period science. If you miss attendance, Ms. Henderson said she'll make you wait in the hall 'til there's a break in the lesson. Could be the whole period. So I gotta hurry. But thanks," I said.

"Maybe I should transfer into science," Kate offered.

I looked at Kate a little funnily. I certainly hadn't made the class sound appealing. Why would she want to subject herself to that?

"I think it's on waitlist," I lied.

I had no idea if the class was full, but I wanted to nip the idea of a transfer in the bud. One class with Kate was plenty.

"I'll see you later," I added, splicing off from her and heading in my own direction.

Over my shoulder, I could see her shrug and head on her way.

I hoofed up the stairs to the science classrooms, but then walked right past my chemistry lab.

Science could wait.

I doubled back down to the first floor via the eastern staircase and looked out into the yard. Kate was right, I fully intended to talk to the janitor, but I didn't need a sidekick to watch while I did. The grass was leaf-free, but the custodian still hadn't moved. He puttered about with his rake, enjoying the sun in the yard. I slipped out the double doors and approached him.

"Excuse me."

He looked up, mildly interested.

"Mmmm?"

"Sorry to bother you, I—"

The warning bell blared.

The last couple stragglers quickened their pace.

I saw that touchy-feely couple from my graphics class saunter up, Greg and Marcy I think were their names. She rode piggyback behind him, her legs casually slung on his waist. They weren't in any hurry. When they saw me and the custodian, Marcy waved. I waved back. The couple went inside. I couldn't help a little jealous pang in my throat. Some girls made relationships look easy. They carried themselves, their bodies, and even their sexuality without a care in the world.

I sure wasn't one of them.

The janitor cleared his throat.

"Oh, sorry. I lost a necklace yesterday. I wore it as an anklet..."

The janitor scrunched his eyebrows together, a nonverbal cue he'd like to stop me right there. I wasn't going to find the answers I sought.

"You kids are always losing everything," he said, almost wistful. Then to me he added, "But I didn't find nothin', don't you worry."

I was surprised. I wanted him to find it so he could return it. Didn't he get that?

"Is there a lost and found?"

"It's in the old wing. But I told ya, I didn't see nothin'."

He went back to raking the nonexistent leaves.

"Right. Okay."

I didn't want to seem rude, but this conversation hadn't gone the way I was expecting.

The older man softened.

"They'll find it," he said to reassure me.

But when I didn't smile or relax, he stiffened up again.

"Have yourself a look if you like," he offered.

He leaned on the rake. It was a beautiful morning and clearly, he had no intention of abandoning his yard detail to help a girl look for a gold chain that he knew he hadn't found.

"Old wing. Lost and found," he repeated.

"Old wing... okay, thanks." I nodded and headed back inside.

Classes were already underway, so there was no point in heading back to the science lab now. Ms. Henderson would probably make me wait out in the hall for the rest of the period anyway. To make me an example.

I decided to find the old wing hallway and check out the lost and found.

I reentered the building's main halls. They were shaped like a letter H on its side, with locker-covered walls flanking the routes to my left and my right. Straight ahead was another shorter hallway. The larger rooms like the cafeteria and gym on the first floor filled in the cavities of the H. The far hallway and back classrooms were the letter's second leg. I could see that part of that hall was shut down with low lighting, and a rope draped over strategically placed garbage cans blocked it off from use.

So that was the old wing.

The building occupancy had shrunk from a full letter H to an upside down letter T.

The classrooms in the back hall were locked tight and unused. Even the lighting was at half-mast to discourage visitors. The second floor, I realized, was a later addition. Up there the natural light and ventilation was better, so the first two floors at the front of the school were now used, while the back half was left silent and empty.

I ducked into the bathroom at the side of the cafeteria when I spotted a teacher supervisor walking past.

The old wing was cordoned off with a rope, so we really weren't supposed to go back there. Although I'd received implicit permission from the custodian, I didn't know if that would hold up under a different teacher's watchful stare. It was clear decisions like this would made on a case-by-case basis and being granted ongoing permission would rest on the whims and the mood of each member of the staff.

Better to avoid another vote altogether.

When the supervising teacher was gone, I slipped under the rope and ducked around the corner. Out of their view, I found myself alone in the closed wing.

As soon as I turned the corner, I knew the janitor was right.

Nobody came back here.

The darkened halls were creepy, and my footsteps echoed.

Here there were other graduating class compilations like the ones I'd seen in the front school hallways, but these framed collections were from further back in time. A quick round of math and I realized my mom and aunt's photos would be here. I scanned the yellowing collages of student faces. As I walked the years back, the photos became more worn and yellowed until I found what mathematically must have been the years the two sisters were in school. I traced our last names with my finger. Only the graduating kids were detailed. Abeline was there. She stared straight ahead, dead in the lens, no smile on her lips, with big curly hair. But there was no Sierra.

That was weird.

Had the family moved on before her graduating year?

I checked the sequence again, but my first analysis was right. My mother wasn't there.

Strange.

To the left, the lost and found box was piled high on the side of the hall. It was full of missing and discarded items, but the custodian was correct, it was just an old dumping ground for things nobody cared about. It probably hadn't been emptied in a very long time.

Still, I went closer.

The container was full of kids' discarded thermoses, their stale and moldy lunches likely still inside.

It had musty, lived-in gym clothes and ratty-looking sweatshirts flush with holes. On top of all the moth-eaten clothing were other useless items like dingy hats with sweat stains and umbrellas that may or may not have been broken when they were initially lost and stuffed inside the box.

Who knew how many belongings were now home to creepy crawler spiders?

I tentatively reached out to pick at the topmost layer.

"Don't touch that."

I jumped a mile in the air, my heart leaping into my chest.

I spun around, and there was Spade, laughing.

"I didn't mean to scare you." He chuckled, but it was plain that he actually did intend quite a jump. "I was kidding. Touch whatever you want."

"I thought this wing was closed." I frowned.

"You're here." He gave me a little wink.

"I saw you duck in and thought you might be lost. I didn't know you were shopping. Ooh, I think this was mine in the fifth grade."

He playfully snatched a red hat off the top of the pile and plunked it on his head.

"I can't believe you just did that. That thing could be swimming with lice."

"Not to worry, I got my cootie shots. Here, you try it."

He played at putting the disgusting hat on my head next.

"Don't even think about it." I dodged out of the way, running headfirst into someone else.

"Oof, sorry, I—"

I expected the janitor, having changed his mind and come to help, or maybe that supervisory teacher intent to stop any foolishness on their watch, but instead, I looked up into another boy's face.

A really cute boy's face.

"—didn't see you."

"Are you alright?" he asked.

His eyes were bright blue under a shaggy swoop of brown hair.

"I'm fine. Thanks."

"We're fine, Beck."

Spade frowned. He slung his arm around me and pulled me towards him like a piece of his property.

"So glad to hear it," Beck said, not sounding particularly glad at all.

His blue eyes flickered over to the lost and found.

"Did you lose something?"

"Oh, yeah. It's nothing,"

I agreed, pushing Spade away. I could certainly speak for myself.

"I just lost my necklace, so I'm looking around."

Beck and Spade exchanged the smallest of glances.

"Well, I could help you..."

"I've got this." Spade interrupted again.

His eyes shot daggers at the taller boy.

"Do you?" Beck questioned, his voice dripping with condescension.

"Really, guys. I'm fine. I don't need any help."

I went back to digging in the lost and found.

"Well, don't go looking." Spade threw a hand over mine.

Beck made a face and picked up the topmost sweatshirt.

He quickly dropped it back on the pile.

"Back off, dude. I said I've got this," Spade snarled.

"Do you want me to look?" Beck asked, purposefully ignoring Spade.

"No, she doesn't."

"I can answer for myself," I told Spade sharply, then added, "No. Really, I'm fine."

Neither boy was looking at me. They were glaring at each other.

What the heck was happening?

The tension simmered.

I wanted to go back to my searching but feared any sudden movement might ignite the spark of rage in the air.

Beck reached down and fingered the red hat that Spade had played with.

"Don't touch that."

Spade snagged it back from him.

"Touch what, touch this?"

Beck tried to snatch it back, but Spade held it physically out of reach.

"How about that!"

Beck clutched a different hat.

Spade grabbed at that one too, but Beck pulled it

back. Spade grabbed a water bottle from the pile and threw it at Beck. He immediately picked up the same projectile and hurled it right back.

"Stop it. Stop!"

I tried to reach out to calm the fire, but the boys were already pushing and shoving each other, slipping and sliding on clothes now strewn out of the lost and found and all over the floor.

I fell in the mess.

"Oh my god, what the hell!"

"Look what you did!" Beck yelled.

"What I did! You're the one who doesn't know when to back the hell off. You're not helping."

"I don't see you finding anything!"

"Get off me." I complained, trying to get out of the fray. "Get off."

"Get off of her!"

"You get off."

Both guys criticized the other, but when they helped me up, it felt more like a tug-of-war than a gesture of goodwill.

"WHAT IS THE MEANING OF THIS?!" Mr. Ambrose bellowed.

The school principal broke up the fight with a red face.

"Pick those things up immediately!"

Spade and Beck muttered apologies and excuses about the other being to blame.

The air shifted in the room from rage to embarrassment.

I felt shocked.

What had just happened?

Where had all that come from?

Quickly, I picked up the disheveled items with the boys.

"Explain," Mr. Ambrose demanded, looking right at me.

"I was just checking the lost and found for an anklet I misplaced when these two lost their minds."

"An anklet. You lost it?" Mr. Ambrose asked.

I nodded.

The principal's face melted back into its usual complexion.

"Right. It's that time again. Did anyone find it?"

"No, sir." Spade lowered his head. "Not yet."

Beck shook his head. "We got a little carried away."

"We're sorry, sir," Spade added.

"Sorry," I agreed.

I didn't really have any reason to apologize for myself, but it was important I speak on my behalf, lest anyone think Spade could speak for me.

The principal sighed.

"Fine. Back to class, all of you."

"Yes, sir." We muttered as a group.

The boys threw the last of the discarded sweatshirts back into the musty lost and found box. I picked up the thermos that had somehow rattled its way down the empty hall and put it back on the pile too.

That's when I saw it.

At the bottom of the wreckage was the tiniest glint of gold.

Grandma Mim's necklace?

I leaned closer, but it was nothing. Just some zipper in a nontraditional metal.

I didn't dare reach for it.

Not in the presence of these bozos.

Not with the glare of the principal on us.

It was a weird glint of gold, but it wasn't my charm.

The custodian was right, my necklace wasn't there.

Where could it have gone?

I gingerly straightened the coffee container so it wouldn't slip off the pile and stepped back. The heap reconstructed, I gave Mr. Ambrose my most sheepish and innocent smile. He nodded and wordlessly led us down the hall. As a group we walked out of the closed wing of the school and back towards the busy classrooms. I maintained a full arm's length from the boys and kept my eyes and hands to myself.

I was not affiliated with them. I wanted everybody to know.

When the hall broke off in different directions, I turned up the stairs to my classroom without so much as a glance back.

When I arrived, Ms. Henderson had finished her lesson, so I was able to slip into the back of the classroom without any further harassment. I got the page numbers for the textbook sections we were working on and cracked open the book, but I knew I'd have to do it for homework. My mind wouldn't stop reeling.

What was their deal?

I was minding my own business, having a little fun with Spade, when Beck appeared, and they immediately descended into a shouting match like petty children. There had to be some bad blood between them.

And why had Spade become so possessive?

He barely knew me.

Sure, I'd been toying with an attraction to him, and maybe he picked up on my immediate chemistry with Beck. But it didn't matter how he felt, I wasn't his property.

I'd barely laid eyes on him.

Something like that had never happened before. I certainly didn't have the looks or the body language that would make strangers fight for my hand.

I wasn't a fan of jealousy of any flavor, but the look in their eyes today had told me there was something deeper going on.

Almost like a power struggle.

My approval was just a weird side distraction.

If I were to guess, the tug-of-war for control between them had been thriving for some time.

Well, I didn't care.

Whatever their weird, macho energy thing was, I wanted nothing to do with it.

IN COMPUTER ART CLASS, everything seemed back to normal.

Spade made eye contact as I entered and nodded a greeting.

I gave a small smile back but sat down at a screen on the other side of the room beside the two Peters.

The boys were conscientious students.

They did their work with little disruption and beside them, it was easy to keep my eyes on my screen. It turned out when I kept my focus solely on the teacher and the task in front of me, I was actually pretty talented at graphic design. At least, I was at this first introductory task.

Kate came and looked over my shoulder.

"I thought you said you didn't know how to do this," she commented.

I had used my photo editing tools to attach a basketball player's head to the body of a praying mantis who was standing at the top of the Empire State Building.

"I don't." I grinned, feeling pretty proud of myself.

"Well, you nailed it," the first Peter agreed.

The other Peter leaned in to see.

"Okay, I give up," he said.

He tilted his screen towards us to show his effort to attach a famous chef's face onto the body of a cockroach sunbathing on a beach.

"Yikes." Kate frowned.

"Kate!" I hushed her.

But luckily, the other Peter just grinned.

"I know who to sit beside in the next test," the first Peter told me. "And who not to."

He looked over at his boyfriend with a grin.

"You can't cheat on a test of skill," the other Peter pouted.

"But you can google it," I suggested.

"Forget you and Peter. My two best friends are copy and paste." The first Peter grinned.

"That's dishonest." Kate frowned.

The rest of us laughed.

"Kate... he's kidding," I said.

But she still didn't seem to get the joke.

After school, Aunt Abeline left a note with two twenties to order myself some dinner. The note said we could eat the leftovers later in the week, but I decided to use the money to fix my bike wheel instead. I figured I could last for days on a toast and butter existence, but I wasn't sure how many more times I could stomach that morning route to school. So, money in hand, I walked to the local mechanic shop, which also happened to be a barber.

In the large front window, I could see a guy in gray overalls was chatting away with an elderly client, a pair of clippers waving around the man's head. They were both entranced in their discussion, but the barber/mechanic didn't seem to be cutting any actual hair. Knowing the size of the town, I doubted there would be another employee in the shop, and I was right. When I peeked into the car bay around back to see if I could spot another worker or a tire patch kit, I had no luck. But just as I was about to double back to the storefront to see if I could interrupt their conversation, someone rolled out from underneath the old, beat-up car on the jack.

It was the girl from the bus.

"You," I blurted.

She raised an eyebrow. She looked at me without any recognition, but she took out one earbud to be polite.

"Josie Jiu."

Her name popped out of my mouth. I was happy to hear myself pronounce it properly.

"You got me."

"I had a dream about you," I blurted again.

What was wrong with me?

What kind of reintroduction was that?

She frowned, getting up off her rolling cart. "Do I know you?"

"No. Well, sort of. We sat together on the bus."

In a big city, this sort of statement would be comical verging on creepy, but how many strangers could she have possibly commuted beside in a small town like this?

She just raised an eyebrow in reply.

"No, sorry. Kate kind of introduced us, but I guess we don't know each other. I'm Mae."

I offered a handshake.

"Josie."

She shook my hand.

When our fingers pulled apart, I could feel grease on my palm.

"Sorry, here."

She ripped a paper towel off the roll on the table.

I took it gratefully.

"You work here?"

"Nah, my boyfriend's dad's the owner. He lets me work on this old clunker. Keeps the customers off his back. They see the full bay and think he's always busy."

"Smart."

She shrugged.

"You need automotive service? I can get him. He's just chatting with Carl."

"I need to patch a flat tire. On a bike, not a car."

She looked over my shoulder.

"Ah, no. I didn't bring it with me. Should I?" I asked.

"Yeah, it depends on the size of hole or the tear. It could need an inner tube patch, or it might not be repairable at all. Wanna show me?"

"You can patch a tire?"

"No, I just wanna look at it for fun." She rolled her eyes.

"Okay, sorry. Thanks."

She grabbed a couple adhesives and glues.

"Which way?" she asked.

"Shouldn't I pay for that?"

"We don't know which one we'll use. Once we identify the issue, you can pay for the materials." She looked at me expectantly.

When I didn't burst into action, she added, "But I haven't got all night."

"Right. Sure. Okay. It's this way."

We walked in silence for a block or two. My guide seemed to prefer it.

Finally, I couldn't stand the silence any longer.

"I'm new in town," I told her, though she hadn't asked.

"I know. Everybody knows."

"Right. Of course."

I could feel us slipping back into silence, so I carried on.

"You've lived here your whole life?"

"Mm-hmm. My whole existence is wrapped up in

this little blip on the map. Geez, could I be more small town?"

"I think you're refreshing," I offered. "My interactions here have been... a little weird."

"They don't have girls like Kate where you're from?"

I clocked Josie's smirk.

That was a direct reference to the bus trip we'd taken together, so clearly she had noted my presence after all.

"I more meant the guys... although the Peters are nice."

Suddenly, I felt her jaunty demeanor turn cold.

Maybe she didn't like the Peters?

"Who's your boyfriend?" I asked, trying to get the conversation back on track.

"You don't know, do you?"

"No, should I?"

I racked my brain, but I definitely hadn't seen her with a guy.

"Not about Beck." She brushed off my silly boyfriend query.

There were bigger things on her mind.

"About the town? About its history?" Josie glanced at me.

When she saw no recognition, she moved on, but I was caught on the first thing she'd said.

Beck was her guy?

This *was* a small town.

I did know a bit about him.

He was one of the guys at the lost and found who'd been acting so weird.

But as for her follow-up question... I knew nothing about the town's history.

Seeing the disconnection between us, she shut down once more.

"Is your house much farther?" she asked.

"Just here."

I hurried ahead and pulled the bike out from behind the storage shed. I wheeled it into my driveway.

"Let's see." She got down low to inspect the hole. "I might need to run a bubble test. You got a bucket of water?"

"Uh, sure. We've got a bucket around here somewhere."

I dug into the mismatched equipment in the tool shed.

"How deep of a container do you need?"

The building was full of gear we'd used once or twice for some specific handyman job some past summer and then never utilized again.

"Never mind, I found it. We don't need to run any air. It's just a simple patch. I got it. All done."

I looked at the bike. It was just as flat as before.

"You need to inflate it," she added.

"Oh. Of course."

She handed it over to me.

"How much do I owe you?"

"It was nothing." She dusted her hands. "But there is something you can do."

She straightened and looked me right in the eye.

"Stay away from Beck."

"Beck?"

I don't know why I pretended to be so uncertain.

"You know him," Josie said.

It wasn't a question.

She was sure our paths had already crossed.

This made me uncomfortable.

"I think you have the wrong impression." I flushed bright red. "We only met by chance and it was barely even that—"

"Don't say chance." Josie frowned. "He's my parabond."

I wanted to ask what that was, but something in her expression told me I should already know what that meant.

"Okay," I said quietly.

I liked Josie. She was gruff and to the point. She said what she meant. If Beck was her guy, I was very happy to steer clear. But there wasn't even anything to steer clear of. I didn't know him, and we'd barely even met. And from what I'd seen so far, he was cute but kind of jealous, maybe a little petty, and definitely strange.

If Josie wanted to claim him, he was all hers.

"We will be... parabonds," she corrected herself. "Once he finds it."

"What's a parabond?" I broke down.

She shook her head and looked at me with pity.

"It's time to have a talk with Mom."

"My mom's dead."

"Oh."

That shut her up.

"Sorry. I didn't know."

I shrugged. It wasn't something you'd tell a stranger the first time you sat together on a bus.

"So you came here by yourself this semester?"

"I live with my aunt."

"And she brought you home," Josie said to herself.

"I would hardly call Plumpkin home... we don't really have one."

But Josie was undeterred.

"Well, she knows. Talk to your aunt. You deserve to know the truth. Before it's too late."

THIRTEEN

LIBRARY WHISPERS

THE NEXT DAY, I rode my freshly fixed bike to school.

I had tried to work up the courage to talk to my aunt the night before.

Josie had hinted at so many curious things, and I felt certain she was right. Aunt Abeline could probably speak deeply on the subject if she wanted to. If only I found the nerve to ask. But when she got home, she was already in a snarly mood.

"Aunt Abby, is there... I don't know... any *reason* you decided that we should move to Plumpkin?" I had asked as I wandered into the kitchen.

From my bedroom, I had heard her come into the front room and bump around.

I didn't realize she was busy stripping bird poop out of her hair.

She was half-cocked over the sink, the faucet

running near her head, runny white sludge slipping down into the basin.

"Huh?"

"What's going on?" I came closer.

"It seems a little bird decided to use my head as a toilet, and look at this."

She tossed the stretched-out corner of her sweater up in the air. A nail or something small and sharp had clearly snagged the fabric, pulling all the fibers in dramatic fashion.

"It's forever ruined. This day was craptastic. Sorry, Mae. What did you ask?" She frowned.

"Oh, that's okay."

She shoved her hair deeper under the tap. Her face was dangerously close to the faucet. White chunks of poop rinsed out of her locks.

"I just wondered..."

"What?"

She cranked the tap off and looked up.

"I wondered... if there was a reason we stayed. Here. Now. In Plumpkin."

"You know me, I go where the wind takes us."

She cranked the tap once more, giving her tainted locks one more blast.

"Yeah."

That was true. It was also maddeningly vague.

When she turned off the tap, I tried once more.

"But was there a specific wind..."

Aunt Abeline squeezed her wet ends in the sink, then flipped back her head. The shock of hair splashed droplets on the kitchen window and drapes. She snatched a dish towel from the stove and furiously wrapped her wet mop into a self-folded turban.

"Mae, what's this about?"

"Nothing. Just something this girl said."

"I've got to blow this out and change out of this." Aunt Abeline frowned. "Then wash the sink to make sure I didn't leave any poop where we eat. Just... give me a minute." She blew past me down the hall.

"Of course. It's nothing. Never mind."

I retreated to the safety of my bedroom and waited.

But after Aunt Abeline's harried arrival, the answers to my questions hadn't come. It was like I'd never asked.

I didn't try again.

I didn't dare to speak the word parabond.

I was too scared. A real chicken.

Truthfully, I wasn't one hundred percent sure I wanted to know what Josie was talking about, and I also wasn't certain that I wanted Aunt Abeline to know that I was nosing around. I had a feeling these were family secrets.

So little she told me.

Why reveal there was something I'd learned? Even if I didn't yet know what it was.

It felt like it needed protecting.

Parabond.

From her or from me, who could really say?

"Did you get back that necklace from your friend?" she'd asked over dinner.

"Oh. Not yet. I was wrong, her date's tomorrow. Or maybe the next day. I'm really not sure. But I'll get it back after that." I barely flinched.

If she could lie about everything in our lives, maybe I could lie too. This time it came much easier.

On the bike ride to class, I daydreamed about how I would get Josie to tell me more about that secret word. Parabond. She'd said to do it before things got too late. But I needed more information than that. Protective as I was around what my aunt did or didn't know about what I had or hadn't heard, I was desperate to learn more.

The bike ride was much shorter than I'd calculated.

My bus route stopped on what felt like every dirt road in the county, but the direct path between my house and the school took only minutes to carve.

I pulled up in front of the building with more than twenty minutes to spare.

I locked the wheel into the metal rack and checked my watch again.

Nineteen minutes and thirty-seven seconds.

Tomorrow, I would add that twenty minutes to my day as a glorious snooze on my alarm.

Most of the student body had yet to arrive.

Having nothing to do on the front lawn, I wandered inside and headed towards the locked door of my science homeroom. The hallways were empty. Since most of the kids were bussed in from neighboring towns, the school population seemed to show up just before the bell rang. As a member of the ride-along gang, I'd never noticed until now. I considered parking my butt on the floor across from the science room, but I remembered all the dust bunnies and crud I'd seen when I searched for my necklace. The linoleum tiles weren't exactly clean.

Instead, I went to the school library.

It was open.

I walked down the hallway and peeked inside the glass wall of windows shedding light on the school's home for the books. There were lots of plants sitting throughout the library and also other kids like me who'd arrived far too early. A few students had books open at the study carrels. Others were typing away on their laptops or phones. And the seats in the library were not covered in grime. They were a solid improvement over the making do on the ground.

I opened the double doors and stepped inside.

The librarian looked up and gave me the warm but phony smile of someone who's being paid to be nice to you. I smiled back and made my way farther into the room. The space was divided into sections. The far right was for fiction. Literary authors and international bestsellers lined the shelves. They sat in alphabetical order with every second, third, or fourth book turned and faced out on the shelf. The titles jumped out, sensationally appealing. That old saying claimed we shouldn't judge a book by its cover, but we all did, and publishers shelled out big money to make their products look as inviting as possible. But I wasn't in the mood for a good book.

I continued my own self-guided tour.

Centrally, there was a class set of desktop computers and a large white screening board. Sprinkled here and there were black pleather armchairs intent on mimicking the comfort and relaxation of reading from home. They were all arranged in little groups of two or three chairs.

I didn't sit down for fear someone else would come join me.

I'd forgone the small talk on the bus, I wasn't about to open myself up to it here.

On the far left of the collection was a batch of study carrels, packed side-by-side in two rows. The wood dividers were tall enough that if you leaned over the desk to work, the only thing visible would be the hunch of your back. Behind those desks were the nonfiction stacks. Eight or ten rows of shelves that were full to the brim with historical, informational, and autobiographical tomes. There was a time when these books were probably a hot commodity for all the research and student projects being done in the high school, but with the easy access of academic papers found online, their printed infrastructure had become more and more obsolete.

Still, they made a great place for hiding.

Tucked in there, I couldn't see anyone, and more importantly, no one could see me.

I made my way into the subdivided categories, my

fingers touching spines as I went. I read the book titles as I roamed, none really catching my eye, until I came across a fairly fat book, a coffee table type of hard cover story, with a very simple title. *The History of Plumpkin Proper*.

Josie had asked if I knew the history of the town.

I didn't.

I pulled the book off the shelf and cracked it open.

But I could learn.

Plumpkin Proper, it turned out, was established in the early 1800s with very little other than a post office and a traffic junction for farmers and tradespersons to pass. While the area was known for its vast array of lakes and waterways, the small town's water supply didn't have any sort of straightforward trade route, so access to the crops via railway needed to be built.

Settler Reuben Plumpkin had laid out the town lots on the lake shores and envisioned a railway running right through its core. People called him the father of the town.

But in the mid-1800s, everything changed.

In 1867, the nearby town of Prince Martin erected the region's tallest grain elevator and investors chose to direct the train station and the traffic into their town instead. With their closest competitor on the rise, the town of Plumpkin dropped the name Proper.

As the years went by, it grew more and more sleepy.

Town planning and population density became

less and less active until one day, Reuben Plumpkin was never seen again.

Presently, the town had never recovered.

It boasted no great industry, and the area functioned as both a farming community and a small tourist destination, depending on if your property was waterfront or sat among the rolling fields. The only other commerce in the community was a large quarry set deep outside of town. But it hadn't functioned in years.

I was about to dig in further than the opening introduction, but the singsong of a couple kids' voices wormed their way into my ear. I hadn't meant to eavesdrop, but they weren't exactly subtle.

"Did you hear?"

Two girls converged on a third friend in the study carrels.

"What?"

"Apparently Beck and Spade Polari got into a fistfight over the new girl."

This set my fire to my ears.

"No."

"Mm-hmm. At the lost and found box."

My mind raced. Some details were wrong, but the gist was correct.

How did other students hear about this?

Would one of the guys have told them?

"I knew it," the girl at the study desk claimed.

"Yup, she's one of them," her friends agreed.

"Of course she is. Why would anyone else come back... wait, what about Josie?"

"Old news." I heard the girl say.

"Jillian didn't say that," her friend corrected.

"Wait, you heard this from Jillian?"

This was disappointing.

The girl in the carrels clearly didn't put as much faith in gossipy Jillian.

"Her cousin told her," the first girl agreed.

"I wish Spade would fight over me," mooned the second teen.

"Uh-uh." Carrel-girl disagreed. "Beck."

"Hands down, Beck," her friend agreed.

The two giggled.

"Oh, Beck would win, but Spade would battle." The third girl sounded wistful.

So I wasn't the only one who immediately saw and felt both the boys' attractive appeal.

Of course, if these girls had actually talked with the fellas about whom they so intently gossiped, their opinions might have changed. But I wasn't about to tell them.

"Have you even seen her?" the study girl wondered.

That was me again, I knew.

Instinctually, I tried to make myself even smaller, but the three girls on the other side of the shelf had no clue I was listening. I hugged the Plumpkin history book to my chest.

"Jillian says she's low level," the first girl criticized.

"Totally plain and boring," her friend agreed.

At the carrel, their friend closed her books and shuffled to get up. "Ugh. They always are."

"Right? Now, if I—"

Suddenly, the warning bell rang out. Three minutes until classes began.

The nosey teens strolled towards the exit, their conversation carrying on. *Probably still rating my appearance.* They drifted off until I couldn't hear them, but I stayed still until I was sure they were gone.

Plain and boring.

Low level.

I guess my plan to sink into the woodwork had been effective.

People always gossiped about the new kid. I knew this. It was human nature. It was something I dealt with everywhere my aunt and I went. Still, it didn't feel great. I shoved the book back on the shelf and made my way to the science lab.

Ms. Henderson did her best to engage me with a lesson about wires and electricity. She even had working light bulbs, which I had to wire myself, and a testing area to experience the shock of faulty wiring issues like connections that sparked and chemical jolts. But my mind continued to wander back to the gossip girls in the stacks.

Being the new girl sucked.

Give it time, I reminded myself.

I hadn't really made any friends in this class, but little snippets of students' personalities were starting to show. Bit by bit, I was getting to know the town, and there would be growing pains while the town got to know me.

There was that quiet girl, Gwen, who was also in my computer graphics course, and the kid yesterday who had given me the homework pages. His name was Reuben too.

Was he named after the founder of the town? Probably.

Parents were that uninventive.

That was just two of the kids, but the town was full of past and present students, each with their own personal stories. Did the nosey gossips chatter about each of them? Tell their stories? Obsess over details? Like what happened to all the other teens who'd filled the lost and found box with their belongings up to its brim? Did they notice their stuff was missing? Did nosey neighbors sit in judgment when they tried to get them back? Each item was a piece of their existence, a token of their family histories, like the moon charm necklace was a part of mine.

It was only natural that a kid would go looking.

Of course, it wasn't the looking that had caught Jillian's cousin's attention.

It was the fighting.

Violence was intriguing, especially if they thought it was fighting over some new girl.

The looking wasn't all that noteworthy.

I doubted that all the beat-up hats and thermoses in that box had even registered as missing. They had carried the holder's family recipes, delicious meals eaten by their clan for generations. They had kept their owners full, and they had kept their children warm, and no one even noticed when they were gone.

Why was I romanticizing a stupid container?

I frowned to myself.

Although it might have seemed like juicy gossip, the lost and found was actually a dead end.

I'd really hoped my necklace might be there.

I'd checked the hallways. I'd checked the classrooms. When I saw that tiny glint of gold at the bottom of the bin yesterday, there was a brief moment when I thought it might be found! But it was just a stupid sweatshirt zipper.

Wasn't it?

Yeah.

Unless it wasn't...

Because of the antics of Stupid Face and Captain Crazy Eyes, I didn't look closely. What if I was running all over the school looking for Grandma Mim's necklace and there it was, in the bottom of that box all along? I should have checked to be certain. But I didn't because there were two lunatic boys and an angry principal hanging on my every move.

Of course, there weren't any stupid boys or principals there today...

I could just check and be sure.

I put my hand up to ask to be excused to the bathroom.

It wouldn't take me a minute.

Two minutes tops.

I'd double check that the zipper was indeed a zipper and then it'd be free and released from the back of my mind.

When Ms. Henderson called on me, I used my teacher exit strategy.

It always worked to get me out of a class: ask a very pertinent, intelligent-sounding question about last night's homework, listen diligently to the teacher's reply, nod politely until the answer was over, and then in the pregnant pause, before they returned to their actual lecture, request a short recess outside of the class. It worked like a charm every time.

My science lab was no exception.

Out of the lecture, I hurried down the stairs, back to the abandoned school wing. This time, I checked thoroughly in all directions to make sure there wasn't anyone around to surprise me or follow me.

The hallway supervising teacher was busy roaming the second floor.

I didn't see any other students.

I felt sure I was alone.

I ducked under the rope deterrent and quickly made the turn into the old wing.

But I was wrong.

I wasn't alone.

Beck was waiting.

"Hi," I said, not actually all that startled to see him.

"Hey," he agreed.

He didn't seem surprised to see me either, like I

was the person he was expecting. But he didn't seem happy to be right.

"What are you doing back here?" I wondered.

"I thought... yesterday... I wasn't sure if I saw something."

"My necklace?"

"Or something else."

I looked at the box. The contents had all been stirred about. It would be hard to find that golden zipper now. I'd have to go through the box piece by piece.

"Well, did you find it?" I asked, coming closer.

"Yeah."

He nodded.

"My necklace?" I looked up, surprised.

"Yeah."

He nodded again. His face was still in a frown.

"That's great."

I stepped towards him. But he held his ground.

"It's not great..." He looked down. "It's complicated."

"What do you mean, it's complicated? Can I have it?"

"If I give it to you, there are... consequences. Do you know about..." He trailed off.

Suddenly, I could guess the right answer.

"Parabonding?"

Beck's frown dug deeper. He nodded.

"You're supposed to 'bond' with Josie."

He nodded again.

"And giving me back my rightful belonging somehow interferes with that?"

I was getting pretty sick of seeing him nodding.

I sighed.

"I'm going to be honest, dude. I'm new here. You all seem to have a pretty good handle on some secret conspiracy, but I have no idea. I've heard the word parabond, cuz Josie said it, but that's it. She didn't define it. It's shrouded in mystery. If you're worried about returning my necklace because you're fearful of some consequences, rest assured, I won't try to hold you to some secret, ancient pact. You're welcome to be boyfriend and girlfriend with whomever you want, parabond, hump like rabbits, whatever floats your boat. I just want my grandma's necklace. It's a family heirloom, my mom is dead, and it's one of the few things we have left..."

Beck looked pained.

I don't know why I played the dead mom card. It seemed a bit overkill. But it did get me the result that I hoped.

He pulled the delicate gold chain out of his pocket.

"Here." He handed it to me.

"Thanks."

I hurried to take it before he somehow changed his mind. I already knew this was the last time I would wear it. I would show its safe return to Aunt Abeline and promptly tuck it in my jewelry box forever. It would never go missing again.

But as the thin little river of gold came back into my possession, I could see that something was wrong.

It looked just like my grandma's jewelry. The clasp and delicate links were an exact match to my mislaid chain... but it was missing the moon.

That beautiful moon charm with etched, layered detail was gone.

The charm on this necklace was a star.

"So that's it." Beck blew out all the breath he'd been holding. "You and I. We're parabonded—"

He raked his hand through his hair.

"How the hell do I tell Josie?" he wondered.

He looked up at me, and for the first time, really saw me.

But I shook my head.

"No... we're not. You're off the hook. This isn't mine." I shrugged.

I'd never seen such relief on a boy's face. It was like I'd just told him I wasn't pregnant. Or maybe I was, but the baby wasn't his.

"It's not your necklace?"

"Nope."

He burst into a huge grin.

"So, I didn't find it?"

"You didn't find it."

"I didn't find it!" He let out a whoop.

"Uh, okay, buddy. Ease up a little. My thing is still lost." I frowned.

"I know. That's such a relief."

"Glad things worked out."

I shoved the copycat necklace in my pocket for safekeeping and dug into the lost and found. I wouldn't bother with hesitation or squeamishness. Today I would check every inch of the stupid, grimy box. I yanked the whole thing onto its side, letting the contents tumble over. In my annoyance, I wrenched the heavy box so hard it smashed on the ground with a sharp thud.

What the hell was his problem?

I didn't look at Beck.

I dropped to the floor and buried myself in the work. I may not know all that much about parabonding, or what the hell that even meant, but if we had been partnered, would that really have been so bad?

Was the new girl really so disgusting?

I dug into old clothes up to my armpits.

He could tell I was upset.

"Hey, sorry. That was rude."

He raked his hand through his hair again.

"It's fine. You got what you wanted."

I pulled out more clothing.

But I just couldn't let him off the hook.

I sat back on my heels and looked him right in his eyes.

"Although if finding my necklace was so terrible, I don't know why you offered to look for it yesterday and why today you came back to dig in by yourself. No one asked you to do that. No one asked you for any of it."

I yanked each item out and stacked it on the floor.

"Seems like a lot of work for a result you didn't want with some low level girl you think is so gross."

I shot him a cold look, then refocused on the task.

This time I'd be thorough.

I wouldn't leave this spot until I'd double-checked through every item and seen the empty corners of the box. Beck could stand there slack-jawed if he wanted. I didn't care who watched.

"I guess I deserve that."

He knelt down on my level and picked up a shirt.

"Sorry. Can I help?"

"I don't know, Beck. Can you?" My biting words stung.

"It's not that I think you're gross or low level," he added. "It's just that I'm already partnered with Josie..."

He gave a sweet smile, but I didn't melt. Seeing my refusal to thaw, he changed tactics.

"I gave you the necklace," he pointed out.

That was true.

He did give it to me, even at what he thought was great personal cost to himself. He could have lied and pretended he'd never found it. I wouldn't have known the difference, but instead he gave it back, knowing there might be a high price to pay.

"You're right. You did." I softened. "Look, don't search. Don't touch anything you might regret. I can do it myself. Just... answer one question."

He raised a noncommittal eyebrow.

"What the hell is wrong with this town?"

He laughed. "I've wondered that my whole life."

We could see I'd gotten the box empty. Unwanted clothing and crap surrounded me in all directions. It was time to put it back inside. I started to systematically pick up each piece, shake it out, check its pockets, and throw it back in the box.

"I'm serious. What is up?"

He picked up a shirt, shook it out like he'd seen me do, and was about to put it back in the box, but I held up a hand.

"I wanna do it myself."

Agreeable, he dropped the clothing back on the pile and sat back to watch me work. He wrapped his strong arms around his bent legs as we went.

"Would you believe... I'm not allowed to tell you?"

"At this point, yes." I frowned.

So far, all I'd heard was a whole lot of nothing, although for such a big secret, it seemed to be common knowledge between every person in town.

"The *thing*"—he leaned in close and checked to make sure I knew what he was talking about without saying any key words—"happens once a year. One new moon that appears like it's full."

I thought back to the unusually bright night I'd taken my evening swim.

That was the day I'd lost my necklace.

"It's kind of a... supernatural pairing. If you bond with somebody, it's your ticket out of town. And, well..." He sat back. "This place doesn't come with too many tickets."

"So you and Josie decided to partner?"

"That's just it, you don't get to pick. The fates make the bonds."

"And you thought fate might have accidentally partnered me with you?"

"Or that this was where I'd find Josie's missing item."

"Only, you found what you thought was my necklace instead."

"The girl loses her stuff, the guy brings it back. That's the whole deal." Beck nodded.

I looked down at the box. Although it was still on its side, it was full once more. I'd gone through and put back every item.

No necklace.

We both stood up and he put the box back on its feet.

"Thanks." I was grateful for the hand, and even more so for the details. It sounded to me like a weird game of hide-and-seek.

He picked up the red hat from yesterday and put it at the very top of the pile.

"What about Spade?" I asked.

"That kid is a turd." Beck frowned. "Stay away from him."

"You can't tell me what to do," I said with a smile, crossing my arms.

"Eh, you seem kinda smart. You can figure it out." He grinned in return.

"Kinda!" I mocked. "I'm a freakin' genius."

We were all done and it was time to go. It had already been *way* more than a couple minutes. This was turning into the world's longest bathroom break. We started to leave together, but I stopped.

"Wait, one more. Why can't anybody talk about... it?"

"There's a history..."

He wanted to leave it at that, but he could tell I needed more.

"You know the Salem witch trials?"

I nodded. "A bunch of kids accused other people of being possessed by the devil."

"Of witchcraft, actually," Beck corrected.

"Right, and there were lots of trials, and..."

"Everybody accused died horribly," Beck finished. "Lots of innocents too. The secrets got out, and... total annihilation."

"Loose lips sink ships," I agreed.

"So they put rules in place to keep each other safe. The first rule: don't talk about it."

"Right." I nodded again, but my brain was still processing.

"Wait. Are you talking about the Puritans? Or the witches?"

Beck just looked at me.

And I already knew the answer.

AFTER MY LITTLE run-in with Beck, I couldn't avoid it anymore. Josie was right. It was time for Aunt Abeline and I to have an honest conversation. It took me a day to work up the courage, but after twenty-four hours of nonstop worry, I was ready.

Witches?

Parabonding?

Witches?!

In my heart, I knew she was involved.

Our permanent arrival only days before the parabonding began was no coincidence. The only real question was how deep did her embroilment go?

Was Mom a part of this?

Grandma Mim?

I wanted answers.

And now, I had an entry point.

The star.

My fingers tightened around the tiny, pointed arms

of the charm that Beck had given me. Technically, it was stealing to take something that wasn't mine from the lost and found, but after all I'd been through, it seemed like a waste to just throw the necklace back in the box. Besides, it looked so similar to Grandma Mim's moon that I wondered if they were a set.

Aunt Abeline would know.

This time, I would get her to tell me.

Waiting for her to come home felt like a personalized version of torture. I sat on the porch... on the deck... on my bed... beside the lake... but no location made time march any faster. Finally, I decided to make a snack. I would cook something for my aunt. I would prepare something delicious. To bribe her into talking... or at least to grease the wheels. I opened the fridge and stared in at the contents. I was hungry for information, not sustenance, so nothing on the shelf was going to answer the call. What I wanted was to dig into the conversation. My fingers touched several jars and containers in the cold, but I didn't pick anything up.

Somehow, things were moving both too fast and terribly slow.

I felt like such an odd man out.

Beck and Josie had their parabonding plan, but who would I partner with? And why was it so clearly determined I would get a partner? I wasn't really part of this town.

The only guy on my radar was Spade.

Beck had called him a turd.

Clearly, he knew him better than I did.

Would I want to partner forever in some supernatural way with a guy I'd just met?

With whom had Aunt Abeline partnered?

And why hadn't she told me about all this?

The treat I prepared for today had to be perfect.

When the fridge didn't yield any results, my picky fingers found their way to our pantry. I opened all the cabinets, peering deep inside. The boxes of baked goods and packages of pasta looked dusty. They'd been sitting on the shelves for ages. Whenever we arrived at the lake house for our temporary holidays in past summers, we just shoved our fresh groceries at the front of the shelves. We'd stop at the local store and get whatever we'd need for a week's worth of supplies, or however long we'd be staying on that particular trip, but there were pantry goods in the back of these cupboards that had sat on these shelves for years.

I pulled an oatmeal cookie mix down and looked over the ingredient list below the fog of dust on the packaging.

Just add water.

A recipe even I couldn't screw up.

A batch of fresh baked cookies was the perfect enticement. It would welcome Aunt Abeline in before I demanded the truth. At the very least, a little nibble myself would take the edge off before she arrived. Plus, it would give me something to do. Left to my own devices, I might go crazy waiting for her to come home.

I wet a paper towel and wiped down the box.

Oatmeal cookies were our favorite. They tasted hearty, but also sweet. You could dress them up with chocolate chips or raisins, but they were also a delicious treat all on their own. I ripped open the packaging and poured the flour/sugar mix out in the bowl.

"Oh my god!" I screamed and dropped the ingredients.

Cookie mix and maggots went flying. The box of powder was crawling full of juicy, white bugs. On impact, a cloud of baking ingredients plumed into the kitchen air, coating my cheeks, clothing, hair, and the nearby cabinets alike.

"Ew, ew!"

I shivered in disgust, but there was no one there to hear my pain. The plastic mixing bowl rolled across the tiles and came to a rest, leaning against the stove.

"Crap," I muttered, coming to my senses after the initial shock.

There was flour and sugar and maggots everywhere.

So much for oatmeal cookies.

I sighed and bent down to pick up the box. Most of the creepy crawlies were still inside. Thank god.

Suddenly, I heard a car pull into the driveway.

Of course this was the moment Aunt Abeline would choose to arrive. This was the opposite of buttering her up. The room was in chaos.

I dove into action to try and clean up the mess I'd just created. I swept the bugs and ingredients back into the mixing bowl, but to no avail. There wasn't enough time to undo the mess I'd made.

"Mae, I'm ho—"

Aunt Abeline breezed in the doorway. She stopped short at the mess. Her face recoiled as she realized the white specks all around the kitchen were moving. "What's going on?"

I looked up from my creepy-crawling oatmeal kingdom and blew a tuft of wayward hair out of my face. The package wasn't perfect, in fact the kitchen and I were both a bigger mess than maybe we'd ever been, but it didn't matter. I couldn't wait one moment longer. I had to know.

"What's parabonding?" I asked.

FIFTEEN
WAIT UNTIL MORNING

"LOOK AT THIS MESS. What on earth happened?"

Aunt Abeline ignored my question and dug into full tidying mode.

I didn't budge.

"I'm serious. What's parabonding? I want to know."

"Just because we want to know something doesn't mean we're ready."

"Just tell me!" I yelled.

It came out much louder than I expected.

Aunt Abeline's face fell. She didn't look my way. Instead, she picked up a rag and started cleaning. Horrified with my own behavior, I dropped my face and my tone.

"No, it's my mess. I'll do it."

I took the damp cloth from her hand.

My aunt stood silently in shock.

"I'm sorry," I muttered, no longer looking up.

Why did I raise my voice?

Aunt Abeline and I never fought.

Although we were a loving extended family, deep down I'd always known I wasn't her direct flesh and blood. She had taken me in as a favor to my mom, but what was stopping her from sending me out again?

"The kids at school..." I said, but I didn't know how to finish that sentence.

I went to work, silently cleaning up the mess I'd made, sweeping the maggots into the dustpan and collecting it all in a bag for the dumpster. Aunt Abeline watched for a moment or two, but when I stepped outside with the trash, she disappeared back into her bedroom, another conversation unspoken, another fight nipped in the bud. I had this mess under control, nothing a few swipes with a damp rag couldn't cure, but the silence told me something else, something bigger and far more fragile had been broken. That was my fault.

I decided to fix it.

"Did you eat yet? I could make us some dinner?" I called down the hall. "Maggot free," I added, trying to lighten the mood in the house.

No response.

I padded closer to her closed bedroom.

"How does that sound?" I asked through the wood paneling. "I'm sorry I yelled."

Still nothing.

I considered my choices.

I could let this go. Give her some time and whenever she reemerged we could pretend it had never happened... or I could push forward.

I knew which one I'd always done in the past.

If I didn't push now, after all this, what would possibly give me the strength?

There were too many questions, too many weird changes.

Talk of witches?

Of bonding forever?

Things were swirling all around me.

I was the only one in the dark, too afraid to ask. Too afraid to hurt my aunt's feelings or tarnish the memory of my dead mom, or... I didn't even know what.

I pulled the star charm necklace out of my pocket. Even in the darkened hallway, the tiny, pointed tips found the light. Their shiny reflections urged me forward.

I found my nerve.

I cleared my throat.

"Aunt Abeline, I lost my necklace," I admitted.

"I know," she said from inside.

Silence returned to the hallway.

"I have something to show you," I told her.

"Come in."

I opened my aunt's bedroom door. She was sitting in the rocking chair beside her bed, staring out the window.

"I'm sorry I lied," I told her.

"Why did you?"

"I don't know. You were starting to open up about Mom and I thought if you knew what I'd done, what I'd lost, you'd think I was too irresponsible to entrust it to. I tried to get it back. I really did. But I've looked everywhere. It's gone. I'm sorry. I know it meant a lot."

"This is all happening quite fast," she said to me with a whimsical smile. She looked both sad and happy. "You're not a little girl anymore," she added and sighed. "What did you want to show me?"

I held out the gold chain with the tiny star charm for her to see.

Her eyes flashed with recognition. She reached out and I passed it over to her.

Aunt Abeline took the necklace, and her thin fingers examined the star's detailed etching like an old friend.

"A boy tried to return this to me," I said.

I watched her closely.

She blinked in surprise.

"But it's not mine. And it's not Mom's," I said. "Is it yours?"

"Yes."

Suddenly, she stood, but then thought better of it. She checked her watch, then settled once more.

"Alright," she said. "In the morning."

"What in the morning?"

"You'll have your answers."

She picked up a book, as if this dismissal should be enough for me. It wasn't.

"Why in the morning? What in the morning? Aunt

Abeline, what's parabonding? I want... no, I need to know."

"Mae, the bank is closed."

The bank?

But then I knew.

There was one thing Aunt Abeline would need the bank for: my mom's safe deposit box.

"What's going on?" I asked quietly.

My aunt gave me a kind smile, then she stood and came over. For a moment, I thought she was going to offer a hug.

I stiffened. We weren't really big on physical closeness.

But instead of an embrace, she put a hand on the door.

"You've waited this long. You can wait one more evening."

Her body language ushered me out.

When I stepped out in the hallway, she gave me a sweet smile and gently closed the door. I was left speechless outside her bedroom door, unsure if I should be insulted at her closing me out or excited by the promise of tomorrow.

I settled on excitement. Dazed, I went back to my room and flopped on the bed.

So it was true.

It was real.

The safety deposit box wasn't just some mythical creature.

I knew almost nothing about it except that it held

all the great family mysteries I had never been told. It would answer all of my questions.

Sometimes, growing up, I had doubted its existence.

How could such a box be the solution to life's biggest concerns?

And if the answers were really mine, why wasn't I ever given a key?

In her final days, Sierra made it clear there were things she wanted to tell me, secrets to be revealed, but I was too little, too young to understand. They would wait until I was older. The plan was a practical choice from a woman with only limited time left on earth and a daughter still too young to hear her mother's precious truths. Though I doubted she'd thought ahead to real-ize, in effect, by pressing pause on all the family secrets, each hidden detail became much more potent. At this point, she was essentially reaching out to speak to me from beyond the grave.

Without that box, those last memories in the hospital were all I had.

Cuddling on that single hospital bed.

I was small as a child and my mom had grown tiny. Being snuggled into her arms while she talked at length with her sister by her side—it was forever my clearest memory of my mom. The rest of my recollections were tainted and swirled with photographic evidence or short stories and anecdotes my aunt had told. Those last few memories were all mine. I cherished them.

I could hear them almost to this day.

．　．　．

"You pass this on when the time is right," Sierra had said, stifling a groan.

Over my head, my mom handed Aunt Abeline a key. She shifted slightly to take the pressure off her side. I wiggled too to help her rearrange.

"Give it to our girl when the moon..." she trailed off, but Aunt Abeline nodded.

"I know when."

My mom sputtered and coughed.

"It should have been you," she told her sister gently.

"Which part? Here? Now? In this bed?" Aunt Abeline asked.

She tried to crack a smile, but both women knew what my mother meant. She tapped Sierra's hand.

"We can't control the fates, now can we."

"No," Sierra agreed.

Then she tucked her chin to look down at me.

"Baby Mae..." She brushed the hair from my forehead. "You'll be so brave."

I nodded.

"You be good for your Aunt Abby. You be patient and kind," she whispered. "You won't be lost." She added, so quietly I could barely hear her, "In my bones, I know... you'll be found."

She'd sung me a lullaby about the moon and the stars, and we promised to never say goodbye.

I fell asleep in her arms.

When I woke up again, her body had grown cold.

She was gone.

After that, Aunt Abeline and I moved into a new apartment. I was crying a lot and I think she thought a change of scenery would help me adjust to a world without Mom.

It didn't, but it did become a new pattern.

We moved every year or two, sometimes later, often sooner.

Aunt Abeline never put down serious roots and by proxy, neither did I. She would get sick of big city life, so we'd take up shop in the suburbs, then the smaller town would feel claustrophobic, so it was back to the bustle of metropolitan life. Nomadic living had its privileges. I got out of a lot of final exams with the moves, but the new lives always took a while to adjust to.

Sometimes it felt like I'd only just settled when we'd take off on another adventure.

Sometimes I didn't bother to settle at all.

I'd asked many times to see the lock box, but Aunt Abeline said it wasn't yet time.

What sort of secrets might it hold?

How could it help me to better understand my mom?

I once "borrowed" the key from my aunt's jewelry box and shoved it into my dress pocket in the same way sometimes kids "borrowed" twenty dollars from their parents' wallet or purse. If Aunt Abeline wouldn't take me, I became determined to go myself.

I visited four banks in town before a manager confiscated the key and insisted we call home. Aunt Abeline had arrived in a rage.

"Secrets are to be told. You can't steal them."

"But she's my mom. I'm ready."

"No, you're not."

"Yes! I am."

The fire in her eyes matched mine and she softened.

"You look just like her," she told me, cupping my head into her side.

"I do?"

Suddenly, I realized I didn't even know what she looked like.

Not really.

All I had were these ugly hospital bed memories and dated, well-turned photos. When I looked for Sierra's face in my mind's eye, she'd become washed in white light. I couldn't picture her. Now Aunt Abeline was saying all I had to do was look in the mirror?

I burst into tears. Big, ugly weeps and sobs.

"Come here." Aunt Abeline wrapped her arms around me and held me while I cried. When I'd regained some composure, she steered me back to the safety of our home.

"The answers will come. Just be patient." she whispered in my ear. "When you're ready, I'll know. But, more important, truly, deeply, you'll know."

· · ·

My eight-year-old self was never going to find that security lock box.

Driving the next day with my aunt, I could see all those years ago I wasn't even at the right bank in the right town. The box was here in Plumpkin.

Of course it was. That made sense.

Plumpkin was the only place in the world with family roots that I'd ever known. Although I didn't remember visiting with my mom as a child, I must have come many times.

My insides flipped in knots.

Aunt Abeline had said that when it was time, I would feel ready.

But I wasn't.

Somehow, even with the overnight wait for the bank to open, the idea that I would finally see what was inside that box made my stomach churn. I didn't sleep a wink. School went by in a daze.

My mom was involved in parabonding. Maybe even witchcraft.

That was crazy.

I was excited to learn more, but also scared of what new knowledge might bring.

"This is yours."

My aunt passed over the lock box key.

We'd barely spoken since school let out. She'd insisted we wait and go get the lock box after my usual day of lessons. I wasn't sure why. I didn't learn a single thing. Getting through each class was agony. Every minute stretched out for eternity.

I turned the silver key over in my hands.

It was attached to a long silver chain. Just gray and ordinary.

I pressed it into my palm. The teeth made a small imprint in my skin.

"We're here."

Aunt Abeline parked the car on Main Street. I looked up at the bank. I expected it to feel mythical, or in some way unexpected. But it was just a cookie-cutter branch of a large chain of banks, like you'd see on Main Street in pretty much any town.

"Go on," Aunt Abeline prodded.

She didn't undo her seat belt.

I was to go in alone.

I unfastened my belt, opened the door, and hopped out on the sidewalk. The town branch looked so mundane, but a whole new world was about to open up to me. Part of me wanted to ask Aunt Abeline to come along.

But to prove my readiness, I didn't dare.

"Hey, Mae," the two Peters greeted me.

I jumped three feet in surprise. I'd been so swept up in my family secrets I didn't even notice the boys headed my way.

"Whoa, easy." They grinned.

I chuckled, my heart pounding.

"You just scared the bejeezus out of me."

"Be cool, fool," Peter said.

"That rhymed!" The other Peter laughed.

"I'm a poet and I was fully aware of the rhythmic

structure of juxtaposing two similar sounding words of disparate meaning."

"Weirdo." The other Peter rolled his eyes.

They looked at me, expecting more banter, but I couldn't engage in their teasing. I was too focused on the task at hand. I looked up at the bank.

"Whatcha doin' here?"

"Huh?" I barely answered.

"Mae, you look like you're about to rob the bank," the other Peter told me.

"What? No. Family stuff."

"Is this you-know-who related?" Peter leaned in conspiratorially.

"Who's you-know-who?" I was confused.

"You-know... who."

"Spade?" I guessed.

"You know who." Peter winked and nodded.

"Stop saying you-know-who," the other Peter complained.

"What? I like it. You-know-who... sounds danger-ous," Peter said.

"It reminds me of Harry Potter."

The other Peter frowned.

"Why've you got to ruin all my fun?" Peter pouted.

"Guys, no. I promise. Just a family thing," I corrected again.

"A likely story." Peter pouted.

But since it didn't involve cute boys or town gossip, I could see they'd lost interest.

"See you, later—"

"—alligator," the other Peter jumped in. "See, I did the juxtapose of similar thingies."

They started to pull away from me and returned to their stroll down Main Street, playfully bickering amongst themselves.

"It's 'juxtaposition.' And you're so predictable. I totally knew you were going to say that."

"You did not. You're jealous I thought of it first."

"You're not the first guy to ever say 'see you later, alligator.'"

"No, but I said it first here, today!"

"Well, *that* is nothing to be jealous about."

"Bye, guys."

I waved them off and hurried into the building before I was spotted by anyone else.

I wasn't about to admit that the family banking I had to do had everything to do with parabonding. Or at least... I thought it did.

Luckily, there was no line for the tellers. I went straight up to the till.

"I'd like to open my safe deposit box," I told the bank employee.

"Do you have your key?"

I held it up for her to see.

"Great. Two forms of identification."

I dug my wallet out of my pocket and offered my birth certificate and government ID.

The clerk looked at the documents then examined my face closely.

"Right this way."

I'd been this far before when I was eight.

This was where, at that other branch, the bank manager had led me to a small room in the back of the building where, instead of leading me to my box in the vault, she'd busted me and made me sit at an empty conference table while she called my aunt.

Today, the path actually led to the boxes.

I had the key.

I had permission.

There was no stopping this.

I was ready.

"In here," she said.

The vault and its rows of boxes reminded me of a community mailbox, with stacks and stacks of slots, enough for the whole subdivision, all in one efficient spot. Only in this room, the contents were guarded by giant locks, thick walls of concrete, and an impenetrable vault door. For extra security, each of the individual containers had two key holes, not one.

"Please." She directed me to one of the smaller squares in the room.

Obediently, I put my key in the first lock.

The teller put her key in the other.

Together we turned the keys, and I heard a small click. The door popped open.

The teller swung the flap wide, leaving the keys hanging on the backside. Inside was a metal box, perfectly sized to fill the slot. She slid it out and put it on the table.

"When you're finished, close the lid of your box, press this call button, and I'll return."

I nodded, playing it cool, but desperate for her to finish with these weird banking formalities so I could finally see what waited inside.

The teller left and quietly closed the door behind her, and suddenly, I was alone.

Everything inside the precious metal cube was about to be revealed.

I had been waiting for this moment my whole life.

Waiting 'til I was ready... and now, all at once, I was.

Ready as I'd ever be.

I took a deep breath and lifted the lid off the box.

INSIDE THE METAL box was one thing: an envelope.

For a moment I just stared at it. My heart pounded. Strange.

It wasn't diamonds or jewels, or a thick wad of cash, but it still had so much meaning. The last person to touch this envelope was my mother. She had placed it here inside this box for me to discover. It had waited here for years for the person whose name was scrawled across its off-white square top.

My name.

In Sierra's cursive handwriting.

Hesitantly, I reached in and picked it up.

I expected it to feel heavy, weighted down with the expectations of a child who'd never really known her mother, weighted with the promise of answers to questions I didn't even know how to ask... although I was learning. Like the first and most obvious: what is a parabond? And how was my mom connected to the paranormal whisperings here in Plumpkin?

But of course, it felt like any other letter.

I turned it over in my hands.

Aside from my name, it had no markings. The lid of the envelope had been folded inside itself, so I didn't have to rip the flap for it to open. I unfolded it gently and looked inside. Two things appeared: another key and a beautiful, ornate card. I picked up the key first.

The gateway to another metal box?

How many safe deposit boxes did my mother have, and why wouldn't she just cram all the information she wanted to provide inside one?

I put the new key down and focused on the card. When I pulled it out of the paper shell, a small picture flitted out of the folds and fell back onto the table. It was my mom in the hospital, sick with whatever had killed her, tubes in her arms, her body in her gown. She looked sick but happy, cuddled on her single hospital cot with a sleeping child nestled into her arms.

Me.

The younger me, fast asleep.

My mom smiled up at the person taking the picture, looking right into the lens, her eyes calm and content. I touched the picture in reverence, but of course there was no more tactile information to gain.

I put it down and opened the card next.

Dear Mae,

Writing to you is difficult. I am gone, but my words remain. How can I ever express all I want to say? We both know I'll fall hopelessly short. But I'll try.

I wish I could be there for so many things. Walking, running, dancing, riding a bike, talking—how I love to hear you talk. The chitter-chatter of your beautiful, small voice questioning everything as you discover the world... I wish I could be there. I would hold you in my arms and send you out with pride on your first days of school, your first date with a boy, and all the future and forever firsts that will come for you still.

You are in my heart, and I am with you in love, every day, always.

You're reading this now, and that very act makes my heart full. You've grown. My darling Baby Mae is now a lovely young woman, cared for so carefully by dear sweet Abeline. Please give her my love. She is a good woman. The best sister to have. You have been raised so well. (Thank you, Abby. Words cannot express...)

Mae, welcome home.

The lake house is a lovely place to land. I suppose you are now learning you have arrived at a crossroads. There are so many things arising as the moon takes its course. I shouldn't speak of specifics, even now, even in death, to keep you safe. But change is coming. The time has come for the fates to decide your path. When you are welcomed into the High Council, you will learn all that your heart desires. If you are passed over, there will be no one who understands that loss more profoundly than your aunt. Deep down, I believe the fates knew all along. They've kept her safe for you so today you two would be right where you belong.

Oh, Mae.

I want to write on forever. How can I say all the words to tell you the love that I have? How can I repay all the kindness, and relive all the moments that have passed?

Baby Mae, be strong and be proud. Whether you're chosen or not, know I love you all the more.

Abby will show you the door.

All my love,

Mom.

Her writing was so clear and crisp. The way her cursive rippled from one letter to the next, there was a river of ink flowing down the page. The art of handwriting was becoming more and more lost, but my mom did it beautifully. Of course, her carefully chosen message brought to mind so many questions.

What fates?

What crossroads?

What door?

Why had she been so sparse in her words?

This was her chance to tell me everything, tell me a million things! She could have rolled on for a thousand pages and I would have studied every single word.

Instead, her message felt almost coded. Like there were things she still held back, even from beyond the grave.

Suddenly, I felt very angry.

For years, I'd awaited this moment, when the doors would fling open, and all my questions would be answered about who I was and where I'd come from — I'd hung all my hopes on the fact that it would all be revealed. But here we were at the proverbial end game, my mother's last will and testament. I'd read every word and I was no further along. This stupid box was nothing more than another clue in a perpetual goose chase. This was my life! Didn't they understand?!

This was my mom!

This was the last message she'd ever send.

I was so sick of the cloak of mystery surrounding it all.

I grabbed the envelope, the picture, the card, and the key, and stormed out of the safe deposit box room and into the hallway. I was done with being careful. My kindness was finished. I had tried to be good and to wait and be patient.

For years. Years!

I'd been the good daughter. The perfect niece and orphan.

But this was too much.

This schmaltz... this allusion to what, exactly?

More hovering.

More secrets.

You couldn't just play with people's emotions. You couldn't just drag them on and on. Families weren't meant to be a bottomless pit of secrets. You couldn't promise a girl her whole life that one day, with one key, she'd discover a world of answers, and then serve her a tepid bowl of nothing... over and over again.

I stormed towards the door, steam practically pouring from my ears.

"Wait! WAIT!"

Someone put their hand on my shoulder, and I jerked back.

I was so worked up in anger at my mom, at Aunt Abeline, at Grandma Mim, and everyone else in my life, I hadn't even noticed the main floor of the bank as I was passing back through.

My arms reeled back, ready to fight.

But I wasn't facing some enemy. It was the bank teller. She quickly retracted her arm.

All eyes were on me.

"Sorry, miss," the teller stuttered. "I didn't mean— I'm so sorry to startle you. We have to close the box together."

She looked miserable.

My anger absolved into thin air.

Of course. Decorum. We had to follow that.

I said nothing but nodded my head.

The commotion over, the others in the atrium drifted back to the banking information and the other mundane tasks that had drawn them to this branch.

"Right." I forced out a smile.

It wasn't the teller I was angry at.

She nodded and led me back into the safe deposit box room.

"I'm sorry for all the formality," she apologized.

I shook my head.

"We take our customer's security very seriously."

"Of course."

My mother's box was still on the table. Wide open.

The teller immediately averted her eyes.

"It's empty," I said sheepishly.

"Yes," the teller agreed, also embarrassed. "Can you—" she signaled that I should close the box and made a big show of not looking.

The contents were supposed to be kept confidential. Even an empty box was no business of the banks. I was supposed to close the box lid and then press the bell. That way it would all be kept secret.

Well, I screwed that up.

I closed the lid.

With the contents hidden, she smiled once more.

"May I?" she offered to pick up the box to return it to its residency.

I nodded.

She slid it back into its wall slot. She swung shut the door. We both turned our keys to lock it in place once more, then pocketed our belongings.

"Do I have to pay something, or..."

I let my voice trail off, no longer clear on expectations.

"Oh, no. The box is fully paid for in perpetuity. Return anytime." The teller gave a soft smile to indicate the proceedings were over. She led me out of the room.

I nodded.

"Is there a bathroom I could use?"

"Of course. Right over here."

She directed me back into the main branch and showed me to the public hall with a guest bathroom stall.

"Thanks."

I forced a smile once more and left her, to both of our relief, to step into the small room's privacy. I didn't need to use the toilet. I just wanted a moment for myself.

The locked bathroom door was a comfort.

I took a deep breath and sighed. My reflection looking back in the mirror frowned. Two minutes ago, I was about to storm my aunt's castle and yell until my knees gave out, but now, all the anger had drained out of my bones. Clearly, my aunt and mom had gone through a lot of trouble to set up this secrecy. The bank had all these finicky steps, pomp and security to ensure my privacy. They probably paid a lot of money for the privilege too. Those were their terms. They had their reasons.

It was disappointing, but it was okay.

I would play their game and jump through whatever hoops were required.

In the mirror, I straightened.

Mom was right.

I'd developed into a mature young woman. I had

grown so much since our last moments cuddling together.

I would make her proud.

I would become the woman she had always hoped.

I would do it all.

But I would do it on my terms.

SEVENTEEN

THE DOOR

"SO, WHAT WAS INSIDE?" Aunt Abeline asked.

I'd gotten into the car without a word.

Of course she'd be curious, I realized.

My mom hadn't told her what would be in the box either. To unlock that secret, she had waited just as long as me. I held up the key.

"She said you'd know what this was for," I said.

Aunt Abeline nodded.

"I do. It's for the door."

She gave me a reassuring smile.

What door? obviously came next, but I didn't ask.

There was more in my box too.

If she could hold out, so could I.

The photo and letter remained tucked in my pocket.

Seeing that for now that was all she'd get, my aunt put the car in drive and took us to what I supposed was the mysterious location of the door... back at the lake house.

Did she misunderstand?

She was supposed to take me to the door.

I'd been through every door in our home. There were barely any with locks. I wanted to question her more, but since I'd started this game of silent chicken, I couldn't be the one to break it.

"Come on," Aunt Abeline said.

She parked the car and headed back into the house.

I followed.

"Help me in here for a minute," she called, already four steps ahead of me. Her voice came from the guest bedroom we basically never used. I followed her in, but a quick search told me what I already knew. There was no secret door to be opened, just the bed, closet, desk, and rug. Aunt Abeline sat down on the bed. She motioned for me to sit beside her.

Hesitantly, I did.

"What was really in the box?" she asked.

I sighed and dug the envelope out of my pocket and handed it over. Aunt Abeline opened it so carefully she must've thought it might disintegrate in her hands. She read the letter and nodded.

"Your mother loved you very much," she said quietly.

"I thought there'd be more," I admitted.

"There is."

Aunt Abeline bent down and flipped the corner of

the rug off the ground, folding the weave on top of itself. Underneath was the hardwood floor.

I looked at my aunt. What was the big secret?

But she dragged the rug farther from its resting place until a small latch was revealed. It was locked.

"What's that?"

"The door."

She waited.

With her blessing, I slipped off the bed and knelt on the wood grain floor. I touched the planks around the lock. What was a keyhole doing here in the floor? This was the door? I took my new key and inserted it into the lock. With a small rotation, I heard something click. I picked up the latch. It opened. When I pulled up the handle, the latch raised, along with a door in the flooring that revealed itself, hidden from view in the slats of the wood floor. The outline of the door fit perfectly with the rest of the wood grain pattern. In the closed position, it was invisible to the untrained eye.

Now I opened it wide.

I looked down the hole into a hallway that dug beneath our cabin.

"Here."

Aunt Abeline slipped a piece of wood under the hinge to keep the door propped open and pulled a string cord. A light down in the hole flickered on. We were looking at a narrow wooden staircase.

"The lake house doesn't have a basement," I murmured.

The house was barely winterized. Its moorings

stood up on concrete blocks above the insulation. If the lake house had a basement, I would have seen it. I would have been in it.

"Come on."

Aunt Abeline went first.

The old stairs creaked as she climbed down. They were steep and led deeper than a regular staircase would. Deep underground.

I touched the dry walls.

The structure beneath the house was sturdy and sound, made of concrete walls. It had been here a long time. How had I never seen it? When we'd traveled two or three floors into the earth, there was another door.

Aunt Abeline opened it.

The staircase led into a small, windowless room.

We were deep below ground level. It was cooler here and felt a bit damp. Again, Aunt Abeline pulled a cord that turned on a light. I expected the space to look and feel like a prison, but the opposite was true. It felt warm and cozy. There was a kitchen table with chairs, a couch with several throw pillows, and a wall of bookshelves with books and knickknacks neatly stored. She turned on two more lights until the room was well lit.

I accidentally brushed a vacant rocking chair. It set off its rocking motion, dust rising as it weaved back and forth in a gentle pattern.

"The place needs to be cleaned," Aunt Abeline noted.

It had clearly been years since anyone had been

down here. But at one time, it may have held heavy use. On the other side of the room, away from the bookshelves, was a small sink and some open shelving. I was also keen to notice there were three more closed doors.

I spun in place, careful not to disturb any more belongings as I took everything in. Finally, I picked up an embroidered pillow from the couch. I ran my finger over the moon and stars that someone had sewn into the fabric by hand.

"What is this?"

"Lots of old buildings out here in the country have bomb shelters and cubby spaces that were built by the owners to keep family secrets. There was a time when this area wasn't quite as politically stable as it is now."

"Family secrets." I nodded. "We must have a few."

Aunt Abeline simply nodded.

I gently moved around the room. I put my hand on the knob of one of the closed doors. When that didn't elicit any signs of distress from my aunt, I opened the door.

"It's a pantry... of sorts," she told me.

I looked at the wire shelves full of glass dishes and bottles. Some racks were full. I pulled the string chain to engage the light like she had done in other rooms, but nothing happened.

"We'll have to get a new bulb." Aunt Abeline shrugged.

I giggled.

I couldn't believe what I was hearing, as if having

to change out a light bulb in one's secret lair was the most normal thing in the world.

"How are all the lights—"

"There's a solar-powered grid on the roof. Bedroom and bath with composting toilet." She continued the tour.

I opened the doors and peered inside.

The bedroom had enough space for a wall of hooks and a single bed. The mattress was dressed with one pillow, sheets, and a quilt folded at its foot. The bathroom was also bare bones. The composting toilet looked a bit like a spaceship, and in the other corner was a small sink. I peeked underneath. As I now suspected, it was self-plumbing. Nothing down here was connected to the house or even the infrastructure of the city. It was totally off grid. The sight of my own face in the mirror surprised me. I almost didn't recognize it. So serious. I forced a smile back onto my lips.

I wandered back into the bedroom.

"What is all this?"

"This was your mom's space. Grandma Mim's before that."

"And now mine?"

Aunt Abeline's eyes darkened.

"We don't know yet," she confessed. "The fates will decide."

The fates.

Mom's letter had mentioned them, and here they were, front and center again.

"Look around," she offered. "Feel at home. Needs a bit of work…"

Home.

As I always did at the mention of home, I looked down at the base of the bedroom door. That's where I would leave my mark. Only I was surprised to see there was already a small gouge cut into the wood.

"No way."

I bent down and touched it.

"Oh, yeah. Your mom used to do that." My aunt shrugged. "It's alright. The door's fine." She strolled back into the larger room.

"I do it too," I whispered, touched.

Maybe in her sacred space, she would hear my thoughts.

I stood and hurried back to the main room to see what else there was to see. My fingers danced over the many textures and items in the room. I didn't know what to explore first. Finally, my eyes came to rest on an old photo album. I pulled it off the dusty shelf.

Aunt Abeline seemed to smile.

I knew I'd chosen wisely.

I opened the album at the table and sat down to have a further look. I began to pour over each photo, trying to take it all in.

"Is that…"

"Your mother? Yes. And me, and Grandma Mim." Aunt Abeline pointed out each person. The photograph was black and white, and the two girls in the image weren't much older than I was today. Their hair bounced perfectly at their shoulders in well-kept bobs. Their clothes looked smart and professional, like they had known it was photo day at school. They looked like little adults in training. The only thing childlike was their smiles. I stared at my mom's grin in the photo. The curve of her mouth looked exactly like mine.

Behind the girls but nearby was Grandma Mim. She stood with picture-perfect posture.

"All these old photos..." I moved further into the album. "They're amazing."

"It was a different time," Aunt Abeline agreed.

I flipped quickly through the pages, trying to absorb all the tiny details at once: high necklines, small buttons on sweaters, the sun catching the leaves through the trees, floral fabric on upholstered couches... then it was on to the next set of images with a fear of missing out, of everything disappearing right in front of my eyes, when—

Suddenly, I stopped.

There was a boy with dark shades on.

He leaned casually on a large boulder, one knee up, a toothpick hanging out of his mouth. Something about the way he carried himself drove straight through my core.

"That's my dad," I said.

It wasn't a question.

Somehow, I just knew.

A sad look came over Aunt Abeline. She forced a thin smile, but I could see she was pained.

"How do you know?" she asked.

"You said you didn't know him."

I ignored her question.

What did it matter, how did I know? I just knew!

But Aunt Abeline wasn't supposed to know. She'd always claimed she hadn't known him, hadn't even known who he was. My father was supposed to be a total stranger.

"Who is he?"

How did she have a picture of him?

"I don't know. It's just a picture of a boy that your mom knew. I figured it was special because it's the only one she had."

"Stop. Just stop. Argh!"

I jumped up, grabbed the small wooden bowl that was sitting on the table, and hurled it across the room. It smacked into the far wall and slapped down to the ground. All these half-truths and unfinished riddles. No one else's family was like this.

"Just tell me! Tell me the truth. Tell me everything! Who is he? What is this place? Why have I never met him? Tell me what you know!" I yelled.

My voice echoed off the walls of the small chamber.

At our feet, the bowl rolled in a circular motion until it settled on the floor with a final shudder.

"I wish your mom was here," Aunt Abeline said.

"Well, I do too. But she's not. Mom's dead."

We both fell silent.

I waited.

This time, I would wait forever.

"Sit." Aunt Abeline pulled out a chair at the table. But I didn't budge.

"Sit with me," she offered again.

Careful to show no weakness, I sat back down. I kept my head held high, anger flashing in my eyes.

She pushed the photo album into the middle of the table, out of reach, and looked carefully at my frown lines. Seeing the something she was searching for, she began.

"After Sierra died, I became your guardian. I wasn't lying, Mae. I've never lied to you. I didn't know your father. I still don't know him. This picture is all we have. You were so young. You weren't ready to hear the family story. I'm not... positive you're ready now. But I was wrong. I let it gather in the shadows. It's been building. I shouldn't have let it get this far. Your mother and I hoped—well, I don't know what we hoped, but you were too young and then she was gone, and things don't always turn out the way we've planned. I thought I'd know. When the time was right, the truth would just come spilling out. I thought I'd know and you'd understand... that there would be a natural moment when it all made sense, when things would come easy... but there never was. Any time I started, the words felt so unreal, so exposed, there was no easy way to let you in. I guess... I started to think you might be better off never knowing. But then I got the letter."

"What letter?"

"From the High Council. Calling you home. And I couldn't avoid it any longer." She stopped.

A million questions had already bubbled into my mind, but once more I waited.

"You deserve to come home," she told me, but it was more of an assurance to herself. "It's the right thing. You deserve to know."

She took a deep breath, the kind of breath you took to build your courage and to access the inner workings and strength of your soul. She looked right at me. Held my gaze. Didn't let me go.

"So here it is. Your mom was a witch. Grandma Mim was a witch. And if the fates allow, in a couple days, or maybe a week max, you'll find your parabond."

EIGHTEEN

NOT EVERYONE MAKES THE CUT

I SAT IN SILENCE.

My parabond.

So it was true.

It was official.

Somewhere in this small town, I was to find my supernatural match. I wasn't sure which words held more meaning, parabond or witch.

"It's not like in the movies," Aunt Abeline offered, as if she was reading my mind.

"There's no broomstick or flying or black cats. It's just a lineage, like any other. It's a vocation, no... a calling. You know how the kids of professional athletes often follow in their father's footsteps? They do really well at the sport their parents played? There's something in that family's bones. A culture to play and understand the game in a way that's deeper than the average fan. It's almost... part of their heritage. They practice, they develop abilities, and they play the same games that their father and his father and his father did. Witchcraft is the same. Some children pick it up really well. Others don't turn out to be very good at the job. Kids like me. I didn't make the cut. I wasn't... very witchy. I don't know. Not like your mom."

She shrugged.

"If you're in, the doors will open. But if you don't make it, there are many things you'll never know. They leave you out in the cold for a reason. For their safety and yours. I was never meant to hold so many secrets. Your mom and Grandma Mim, they were in. Even Grandpa Charles. But I was out. I was alone."

Suddenly, I saw the pain she'd been through.

Aunt Abeline wasn't holding all the answers. She only knew there was a fantastical path she hadn't followed. I thought being on the outside of the family secrets for a few weeks was painful. She'd been locked out her whole life.

"That might be you too," she added, as if guessing correctly about what I was thinking.

"You might never get answers. If you don't parabond..." she drifted off. "Or, maybe you will," she added. "I don't know."

"But what about him? My dad. He was a wizard?"

"From what I've gathered, yes. I think your parents were parabonded by fate and then sent to train at the High Council together. That's how they met. After that connection... if you parabond... you'll be transferred to another place. High Council. I don't know much about it."

Because she never went, I realized.

"Everyone gains access in the same lunar cycle. When the fates think you're ready, they strip something of value from your person and find a worthy person to retrieve it and bring it back to you. They're your parabond. That's it. The whole thing is kind of subconscious. You don't even know it's happening until it's happened."

"This girl on my bus says she'll parabond with her boyfriend."

"That happens," my aunt agreed. "Sometimes. But there's no way to call your shot. It's the fates who decide. And you only get one attempt."

"What does that mean?"

"Well, for some kids, it happens right away. For some, it takes a couple years to warm up. There's no set age where fate intervenes, but once it does... that's your only chance."

"So when I lost Grandma's necklace, you knew that was the universe beginning the process. If it's gonna happen for me, my para-boyfriend is now on his way?"

Aunt Abeline nodded.

I frowned. If only dating were that easy.

"That charm necklace has gone missing and returned before," she agreed. "And of course, I had the other one just like it," she added.

"With a star instead of a moon," I agreed, "which I found. Well... Beck found it. But I'm the one who gave it back to you. Maybe we'll parabond?"

"I'm afraid it doesn't work that way. That's the last rub. There's an expiration date." She used her hands to motion the ticking of a clock. "New moon, waxing crescent, waxing gibbous, then it's done. The full moon is the final call. If your possession isn't found quickly, it likely won't be found at all."

She dug out her gold chain and laid it out on the table before her.

"I lost this one year after your mom lost hers, but no one ever brought it back to me. I was rejected. They don't say anything, the High Council... no one does. The silence might be the worst of all. And your mother couldn't tell me about it. It's a secret society complete with its own heavy rules. The only thing I figured out on my own is, much as it might seem it, the parabond isn't really a romantic attachment. It goes much deeper. You are permanently tied together. Like a yin and a yang. Whatever choices they make, you have to live with them too."

"We're not supposed to know anything about this, are we?"

Aunt Abeline shook her head.

"The fates remain uninterrupted, but the process has become corrupt. Believe me, when we arrived back in town the whole place knew there was fresh meat. I fielded a lot of phone calls."

Some even in the middle of the night, I remembered.

Fresh meat.

That's how they saw me.

My aunt was right.

I thought about the two boys who'd fawned over my missing necklace. There was nothing organic about that.

"Maybe my charm's lost forever." I shrugged.

The whole thing seemed forced and creepy.

"Don't say that."

"They didn't find yours, and you turned out."

"Mae..." She struggled.

I could see her wheels turning. Perhaps she thought she didn't turn out.

Perhaps not parabonding was her biggest regret.

Or maybe she just wanted to do right by my mom.

"If you want to know your mother, really know her, you're going to have to go where she went, do what she did. The choices she made, the pressures she felt... This was it. This was her whole life. How else could you possibly understand?"

That wasn't fair.

It wasn't my fault she lived a secret life.

It wasn't my fault she died when I was a child.

"Don't be afraid."

Aunt Abeline looked wistful.

"If the fates do align, it's a gift. And your mom would be so proud. Sierra was happy to be a witch. Grandma Mim too. I was the odd man out. It's a special opportunity to become everything the universe intended. The fates won't provide if you can't carry the load."

"Thanks, that makes me feel better," I agreed.

But I hid my true evaluation.

I didn't want my whole future to be pinned to some guy who was good at the game of hide-and-seek. If the fates were going to welcome me into the High Council chambers, I would enter them gladly, but it wasn't going to be as arm candy as some parabond's date.

I would do it my way.

I would find my own damn necklace.

And I would do it alone.

I WOKE up early the next morning, ready for action.

The first step to finding my necklace would be to retrace my steps. Going above and beyond walking my original route, I wanted to copy everything that I'd done on that very first day. Maybe it would jog a memory.

When I came out for breakfast, Aunt Abeline was at her regular spot at the kitchen table, a mug of coffee in one hand, her laptop in the other.

A million family secrets had been revealed over the weekend, and yet she barely blinked at my entrance. I would almost never have believed the details of our discussion if not for the floorboard key in the keepsake bowl on my dresser. That, and Aunt Abeline's star charm necklace was now back around her neck.

"Ready for school?" she asked in passing, her fingers floating to the thin metal chain.

"Breakfast of champions," I nodded.

I popped my double-toasted piece of bread out of the toaster and plied it with butter.

The gates of communication should have burst open after all our secrets had been revealed, but the practice of silence was deeply ingrained in us both. I hadn't told my aunt that I planned to recover my own object. I wasn't sure if she'd approve of my taking fate into my own hands. Surely she'd thought of it when she'd been the one involved. Who would sit and wait for a fortnight, their fate so totally in someone else's control?

But she never mentioned it.

Who knew what other thoughts and feelings my aunt still wasn't sharing?

"I hope things go well," she said, her eyes giving off a small twinkle.

"Fingers crossed," I agreed, although it was very possible we both meant different versions of the same result. "Thanks again... for sharing," I added awkwardly.

Aunt Abeline waved off my gratitude, her eyes already refocused on her laptop screen.

Baby steps.

While still swallowing, I headed out.

I grabbed my bag and made my way to the school bus stop. I could ride my bike now, but I wanted to be extra thorough and check every nook and cranny of the public transit. It was part of my retracing plan.

Maybe I could even get more details out of Josie.

Besides, I didn't have long to wait.

The big yellow bus pulled up on time just like it had every other day.

More at home with the routine, I bypassed unpleasant conversation with the driver and made sure Kate could see me wearing my headphones and pointedly checking my phone. I gave her an exaggerated nod and then stared deeply into the tiny screen, clicking digital buttons, making it clear I wouldn't be chatting during today's ride. I sat on the same bench that I had that first morning and settled back into the seat. When I was sure no one, not even Kate, was looking, I took out another beaded anklet and fastened it over the bones of my foot. The little glass balls brought just a touch of sparkle to my ankle. Perhaps wearing this new jewelry would give me a better sense of where I'd been and when the original charm necklace might have fallen off. It was worth a shot anyway.

I put my bag on the seat beside me to discourage new seatmates.

There was only one person I wanted to sit beside me today.

"Josie!" I waved when she boarded the bus.

She looked down the row of seats to see who was calling, but instead of making her way back, she sighed, turned, and plopped herself down in the very first open chair.

So much for reenacting everything from the day the necklace had gone missing.

Of course, on that first day, I hadn't known her name.

She'd heard me, I had seen her hesitate for a moment, but she chose to sit as far away from me as possible.

Maybe Beck had told her about our lost and found connection.

Or maybe she didn't want to babysit my unanswered questions.

I knew so much more now. But she had no way of knowing that.

Maybe the girl just didn't like me.

Either way, my invite was clearly declined.

"She's so weird."

Craning around in her seat, Kate rolled her eyes.

Kate and I also met that first day. In fact, she'd talked to me over the back of the bus seat then just like she was talking to me now. Maybe this would help with my reenactment.

"Yeah, lots of weirdos around here." I shrugged.

I made sure to offer her a rueful smile to let her know I didn't lump her in with that lot.

"Why are you still bussing?" Kate asked. "I thought you got your bike fixed?"

"Word travels fast." I laughed.

What a weird thing to get passed through town gossip—the new girl had her bike patched.

Riveting.

Kate shrugged, but I could tell she really was curious why I was back on board.

"Old habits die hard," I said, shrugging.

It was a poor excuse.

Any kid in their right mind would want off the bus for good, but Kate didn't seem to notice.

"Well, I like the bus," she reminded me.

"So you've said." I smirked and rolled my eyes when she wasn't looking.

Then it hit me—she really had said that exact phrase before.

Just then, the driver applied the brake and made a sharp turn into the school parking lot. I grabbed the back of the chair to stop from falling over. That had happened before too.

I was right.

My reenactment was starting to work.

This was beginning to feel like déjà vu.

"We're here," she said.

"So we are..." I agreed out loud, playing my part with accuracy, just in case.

I looked down at my ankle.

My beaded loop was still in place. If it was already lost that would be too easy. I got off the bus and took in the schoolyard surroundings. Kate had gone on ahead and I was glad for a moment to myself. The crowds on the front lawn were different than the first day. It wasn't an exact replay of that morning, but I had managed to recreate a couple weird coincidences.

I put my bag up on my shoulder and headed towards the front doors of the school. Now that I knew some of the truth about this town and my family's history, I couldn't shake the feeling that there were a lot of eyes on me.

Aunt Abeline had called me fresh meat.

The High Council had actually beckoned me. Everybody knew it.

Now that I'd arrived, how many people were watching the show?

Who knew I'd lost my anklet?

What other teens were hoping to get in?

And maybe the most important question for this particular situation: when it came to the tickets to the High Council initiation, how short was the supply?

Pretty short, I realized.

There were only a few entrants each year. That's why when the boys learned I'd lost something, they lost all common sense. They were competing for a spot.

If Aunt Abeline hadn't gained enrollment in her year, if she wasn't accepted, it stood to reason there would be others who would be rejected in this year as well.

If I got in, perhaps another girl would miss out.

There were only so many spots to go around.

Josie had warned me to stay away from her man. That wasn't petty jealousy, that was self-preservation. He was her ticket to the High Council. The only way she could enter.

Well, she should know I wasn't her competition.

Out of the corner of my eye, I saw her with Beck. His arms were wrapped around her shoulders.

I steered my route to a farther path.

With him by her side, now wasn't the time to start a conversation. Both looked up at my passing, even across the quad. I formed my mouth into a tight smile to show I meant no antagonism. She turned his head away from me and pulled him in for a slow, deep kiss. Beck's hair fell across his forehead as he bent down into her embrace. His hands casually roamed her body and traveled down her back to her jean shorts. He thrust his hand into her back pocket, cupped her bottom, and pulled her towards him, deeper into the kiss. When they came up for air, his eyes drifted over her head and caught my stare. I quickly looked away.

That should have been it, but I couldn't help myself.

I peeked and found Beck in my peripheral sight again. He had turned their torrid embrace into a comforting cuddle. He held Josie close, her head tucked up under his chin.

Again he caught my eye and offered a small smile.

I smiled back and let myself disappear into the schoolyard fray.

Would it be so bad? I asked myself as the day wore on, not listening to a word the teachers said.

Being parabonded?

Josie and Beck seemed really happy.

My aunt had said it wasn't a sexual connection, but what did she know? In the game of the High Council, she'd never arrived at first base. Josie and Beck certainly seemed connected. Not that they'd parabonded. Or maybe they did? I had no clue how they did or didn't. Or how often they... connected. It was really none of my business. So why did I keep thinking of them?

I blushed at the thought of that kiss.

Beck's kiss.

I wanted to be kissed like that.

When we lived in the city, here and there, I'd dated a little. Mostly I roved around town in a large group of kids. Some mediocre boy would invite me to hang out with his friends and I'd go along because that's what kids did. I'd had a few kisses and held hands in public situations, but the touch of those boys was nothing like the grip of Beck's hands.

I wanted a set of those hands for myself.

"Mae! Hold up a second. Mae! I've got something for you."

As I entered the building, I could see Spade had been waiting for me, chatting with a couple of seniors by the lockers, with one eye on the atrium hall.

Shoot.

When I said I wanted hands on me, I didn't mean Spade's.

He tried to wave me down.

I slipped to my left, pretending not to hear him.

Unlike when I'd rode my bike, arrival on the bus put me smack dab in Plumpkin's biggest bottleneck. I dodged and weaved amongst the kids heading to first period. Spade called behind me but if I didn't sway my head, he'd never know that I was ignoring him on purpose. I was fortunate that from my attempt to deter Kate, my earbuds were already perched in my ears.

He had something for me?

Could it be my necklace?

I wasn't about to stay and find out.

I popped into a first-floor math class with two exterior doors. I found myself in a classroom full of freshmen. Several sleepy-eyed teens looked on with curiosity as I hurried from one entrance to the other. I yanked open the second door and stumbled back into the hall, cutting through a group of seniors who were used to hanging in the little alcove the second entrance provided.

"Careful, girl." The taller boy with dark skin and beautiful, heavy lashes frowned. His blonde friend just smiled.

"That's what we get for standing in the door," she said. She hugged her books to her chest to let me pass.

"Sorry... sorry."

I peeked up and down the hallway. My little double back through the classroom had worked. Spade was now in front of me heading farther in the wrong direction.

I breathed a sigh of relief and walked right into Kate.

"Mae, what are you doing down here? Don't you have science on second?"

She was delighted to see me.

I just wanted her to keep her voice down.

But it was too late. At the sound of my name, Spade turned.

I ducked my head, but not in time. He'd seen me.

"Mae!"

"Gotta run. Don't wanna be late," I told Kate, pretending I didn't know Spade was jogging to catch me.

She looked from my departing back to Spade chasing after me.

I lurched into the main floor stairway.

This wasn't right. I shouldn't be running through the halls. I was doubtful that I could make it to the second landing before he caught me. I considered turning to face the music, but just then, the Peters strolled in from the exterior door.

"Hide me," I said, throwing myself at their mercy, ducking behind them in the low overhang of the stairs.

The boys had barely a moment to think before Spade burst into the stairwell. He looked wildly up the stairs and out into the courtyard, trying to decide which way I'd gone.

One of the Peters *tut-tutted*.

"What bee's in your bonnet?"

"I'm looking for Mae," Spade said.

In tandem, both boys pointed upstairs.

How they knew to do that without any discussion was incredible.

"Thanks." Spade jogged up the stairs two at a time.

"Welcome," Peter called after him.

"Where do you want to go for dinner?" the other Peter wondered.

"Ooh, what about Chinese?"

"Oh, please."

Upstairs, we heard Spade burst through the second story fire door.

"There's a Chinese restaurant in Plumpkin?" I asked, coming out of hiding.

"No. That's why it's such a stupid joke." The other Peter rolled his eyes, but his boyfriend was very pleased with himself. "Now spill."

"Why are you hiding from Captain Dreamboat?"

"He was trying to give me something." I shrugged.

"Give? Or return?"

Both Peters raised an eyebrow.

"Not you guys too."

"What do you mean, not you too? Don't think the gays can parabond?"

"That's not what I meant—"

"Cuz we can't."

"Well, we never have."

"And we won't."

"Why not?" I asked.

"Oh, who knows? It certainly doesn't run in either of our families."

"I'd tell you if it did," Peter told the other Peter.

"And I'd tell you!"

The boys both grinned at each other.

"For a secret society, the town sure does talk about this a lot," I muttered.

Both Peters turned their smiles on me.

The other Peter disagreed. "I don't know, sweetie. For you, that's true. But not for me."

"Or me. Had you ever considered, in all those talks, that whole plethora of discussions, you're the common denominator? We're not losing or finding anything."

"Good word," the other Peter complimented. "Plethora."

"I speak good vocabulary."

"Huh." I considered this. "Has anyone ever told you that you two are very, very smart?"

"And handsome," Peter agreed.

"I don't think we hear it enough," the other Peter added.

"We really don't."

They grinned.

"So, you don't wanna match with Spade?"

"I don't want to match with anyone," I said.

"With any man?" Peter ventured.

Was there something else about my orientation that they should know?

I shook my head.

"With any strange guy. Think about it. Agreeing to a partner forever? It would be nice to have spent a little time getting to know your new lifelong friend. What if I don't even like him?"

"I dunno. That's just the way it works."

"Why?"

"How should we know?"

"Right," I said, remembering.

No one knew anything in this town. It was just fate calling all the shots.

"You'll figure it out," Peter softened.

Just then, the warning bell rang. Other students opened the hallway doors and made their way to first period.

"We should get to class," I noted. "But Peters..." They both turned. "Thanks for covering."

"Aww, Mae."

"You'd do the same for us."

My first two periods went by in a blur. I hadn't lost the bead anklet from atop my foot, and I was no closer to enacting a plan to get into the High Council myself. I couldn't stop thinking about how Spade might already have my necklace in hand. The only way to delay the inevitable would be to make sure he couldn't find me to give my item back to me. I decided the best way to do that was to skip computer graphics class altogether, so that became my plan. Only, as I exited my period two lesson, I ran straight into Mr. Hanks. He was headed in our class direction.

"Ms. Kingsley." He gave me a warm, teacherly smile. "Are you settling in at the new school?"

He fell into step beside me.

"Oh." I nodded hello.

I looked longingly in the other direction, but to pull away from my teacher and skip out on his class completely while he was literally walking beside me would be awfully rude. I just couldn't pull the trigger. Resigned, I fell into step.

"Things are going okay, thanks." It was a generally positive non-answer.

Together we rounded the corner and stomped

down the stairs. As we passed the doors to the outside world, I seriously considered the exit, but there was no way to extricate myself gracefully.

"When Mrs. Barathavich mentioned you didn't have the prerequisite for graphic design, I was a little worried about your pace with the class, but you're picking up the program like a natural," he encouraged.

He held the door open for me. We walked through together.

"Yeah, I actually kind of like it," I agreed.

Before we even entered the classroom, I could see Spade was waiting to chat.

I hugged my books to my chest.

"Actually, Mr. Hanks, I have a couple other questions," I said, swerving past Spade, keeping pace with the teacher.

"Oh?"

I followed him to the front of the class and kept my back to the rest of the students.

"Yeah. If I were to go into graphics in postsecondary education, what other courses should I take?" I asked.

Teachers loved talking about your choices for future schooling. It was like once they had you here, in their classroom, they couldn't get enough. They simply loved learning. Once you opened a conversation about opportunities at the postsecondary level, some of them never shut up. I figured if I could monopolize Mr. Hank's time right up until the late bell, then Spade would miss his window to talk to me.

"It's good to hear you're thinking about your future, Mae. There's a whole list of electives you should consider, starting with communications technology. Visual art is also a great compliment to our graphics elements. You'd think they don't go together, but a lot of the visual representation we make on the computer, visual artists were already doing with pen and paper. There's a lot of theory to be learned."

I nodded.

"Visual arts... got it. Although I'm not super great at drawing," I admitted.

"Well, it's like any skill: you practice, you grow." He grinned, organizing his papers.

I hadn't considered that art was a skill you could learn and get better at. I'd always figured you either had artistic genes or you didn't.

Like entering the witchdom.

I snuck a peek at Spade. I was running out of steam to keep this conversation going until—

Just then, the class bell rang.

Victory.

Class was starting.

"I better get things going," he told me.

I nodded and left the teacher's side and headed back to my desk.

"Still avoiding Spade, I see," Peter whispered under his breath.

I grinned as I sat down.

"I didn't think we'd see you," the other Peter added.

"I got pinned by Mr. Hanks in the halls," I admitted. "So, I improvised. Now I only have to get the hell out of—"

Peter's phone trilled. He absently checked it while I was talking.

"Uh, Spade just texted."

All three pairs of our eyes bugged out of our heads.

"Why didn't he text you?" the other Peter wondered.

"He doesn't have my number." I shrugged. "No one here has it."

"Aww, sweetie. I'll take your number," Peter offered. "Put it in here."

He passed me his phone.

"Okay."

I threw my number into Peter's phone.

"Me too," the other Peter added.

With equal quickness he forwarded a message to both me and the other Peter so we would have each other's numbers too.

I leaned forward.

"What did Spade's text say?"

"To tell you to hold up after class, he has something for you."

"Well, pretend you didn't get it."

The Peters frowned at me.

"Or you did but you didn't want to give it to me," I suggested desperately.

"Uh, no. I'm not taking your heat. Whatever this is,

you've got to clean up your own mess." The other Peter shook his head.

"We don't get in between a lovers' quarrel. You should have seen this one time our friend Jade broke up with this guy, Pete."

"You had another friend named Peter?"

"Uh, no, his name's *Pete*," the other Peter corrected.

"That's not the point of the story." Peter wouldn't get derailed.

"And we weren't friends."

"Just, would you let me tell it?"

"Alright, tell it already. I could have got to the point like seven times."

"The point was, she didn't want anything to do with him, so when he was coming over to see her, she asked me to stay sitting beside her in an assembly, you know, the one for drunk driving where they tell the sad story, and everybody feels bad about irresponsible drinking but then just keeps on irresponsibly drinking anyway?"

Peter and I both nodded.

I'd seen that same morality film at every school I'd ever attended.

"Anyway, he comes over, all sweet-as-pie, and asks to switch seats. When I said no..." Peter shuddered, remembering. "He called me a pig-faced fag boy."

"Stop giving people what they want, they can get real dark, real quick," the other Peter agreed.

"Right. Sorry. Of course. I get it. Geez, that's gross.

That wasn't fair. It's my problem. I'll deal with it," I said.

Both Peters gave me pitying smiles.

"Just get it over with," I muttered to myself, and I didn't have long to wait.

Mr. Hanks introduced a group project. For the next class assignment, we were all supposed to work together in pairs.

"Wanna work together?" Kate broke into my thoughts.

"What? No. What?"

I looked blankly at her.

I'd been so lost in thoughts about Spade I didn't even hear her properly.

She laughed.

"Question two to five... the list on the board? We need partners."

"Oh, right." I shook myself out of my stupor.

"She's already partnered with me." Spade swooped in by my side.

I looked up at him, this time not surprised. He gave me the tiniest of winks, then delivered Kate his most winning smile.

"That's right," I agreed. "Sorry, Kate. Another time."

She shrugged and moved on, looking for another victim.

Spade plopped down beside me.

"You're welcome."

"For what?" I shrugged. "Kate's not so bad."

"And yet, given the chance, you turned her away?" He grinned.

Busted.

"Well, Pete told me about your text." I nodded and shrugged. "Don't take it as some big, meaningful thing. I'm not even sure I like you," I told him honestly.

He laughed.

It didn't cross his mind that it might be true.

Spade was used to being liked.

"I have something for you," he whispered.

"What?"

My eyes grew wide. This was it.

He grinned, ear to ear.

I felt the breath catch in my chest. Deep inside, I could feel a tightening knot.

He made me wait one beat longer, then pulled out the red cap from the lost and found. He tossed it on my desk and wiggled his eyebrows.

"This... is for you."

"That's not mine," I said. I let out the breath I didn't know I'd been holding.

"Pity, I like a girl in a ball cap." Spade shrugged. "Try it on," he offered, picking it back up.

"If you try to put that thing on my head, I will seriously never speak to you again."

"Fine."

He plunked the hat on his own head and gave me a sloppy grin.

I rolled my eyes, but this was how I liked Spade

best. Sweet and goofy. Plus, he didn't have my necklace. We were just fine.

"Shall we?"

I looked around and realized the other partners in class had started wandering out into the halls.

"What are we doing?" I asked, happy to follow along.

"Oh man, where have you been?!"

"Nowhere. What? Just around, like usual."

"You're so distracted. Is it me? Because I am into it. You're somewhere between a city girl and a country mouse and I am in."

"Oh yes, Spade. I want you so badly." I gave him my most deadpan retort. "Can we please just do the assignment?"

"Sure. What is it?" he teased me.

"Where's Kate?"

I pretended to leave him, but he pulled me back.

"Alright, okay. You're a tough nut to crack."

"Have you even tried?" I asked, shooting him a dark look.

He seemed surprised.

I shoved open the school double doors and burst out into the sunlight, pulling a stride or two ahead. He followed.

"Okay, I deserve that," he agreed, falling into step with me.

I marched ahead, unsure where I was going, or what I'd do when I got there, but determined to leave him behind in my tracks.

"Wait, Mae—" He reached out a hand to catch me. "You're my partner."

An electric shock snapped through us both where our skin touched.

"Ow!" I said.

We recoiled in surprise. The spark was enough to stop me from walking.

"Wait," he repeated.

He brought his hands up defensively, afraid to touch or shock me once more. His expression changed.

"You know, don't you?" he asked.

I shoved my weight onto my other hip.

"You didn't, but now I think you do."

"Know what?"

I crossed my arms.

"We're... a match."

"Did you find something? A *real* something?" I asked.

"No."

"Then I'm not matching with anyone." I shrugged and turned away.

In the courtyard, our classmates were starting to take pictures of one another.

"Not even Beck?" Spade asked defensively.

It dawned on me suddenly that with all this parabonding talk, there was pressure on the girls to be found, but also on the boys who had to act. They had to find the items in a timely fashion and bring them back to the right person. The girls waited passively like a toy on the shelf, but the boys had to find the dumb things. I had spent an hour or two this morning looking for my necklace and I was already stressed to pieces. Who knew how long Spade had been on the hunt to find his partner's special thing.

"I don't even know Beck." I rolled my eyes.

"Right."

Recognition flashed in Spade's eyes.

I hadn't denied it and he noticed.

I thought about adding an extra rejection just to drive it home that Beck and I were not connecting in a paranormal sense or otherwise, but what was the point? I wouldn't partner with Spade either.

He frowned, then forced himself to smile it off.

"I just realized I left my cell phone inside," he told me, backing away.

"What are we supposed to take pictures of?" I asked.

"Your idea of beauty!" he called over his shoulder, then jogged back inside.

I should have paid more attention in class.

I pulled out my own cell phone camera. I flipped the viewfinder to its best photography mode and scanned around the outdoors through the lens.

My idea of beauty?

Nature was full of it.

I could take a picture of some trees and stuff. It wouldn't win any awards, but I was just trying to pass. I checked to see if any of my classmates had had a similar idea, but they were mostly just hanging out in the sun, using the excuse to flirt with each other and check their social media accounts.

I wandered under the giant courtyard maple tree. The branches were thick and sturdy. It had been growing untouched for several decades. Here underneath its shade, the grass was dark green with just a touch of sunlight trickling through.

I looked up.

The sky looked deep blue behind the green-and-brown crooked branches. It was a beautiful angle. I lay down on my back to get a better view. Sunlight filtered all the way into my frame. I snapped a couple photos.

Suddenly, I felt a chill.

The hair on my arms stood on end.

I sat straight up and looked around.

It felt like I was being watched.

No one's eyes that I could see rested on me, or even seemed to be paying attention, but I got up quickly from the ground and dusted myself off. I checked back towards the school building.

Maybe it was Spade on his way back to me?

But in the doorway, I could only see Kate.

When she saw me looking over, she waved, then disappeared inside.

My eyes floated upwards to the second story window. It was empty, but I couldn't help the feeling that a moment before, someone had been there.

TWENTY
PARABONDING ON THE LAWN

WHEN SPADE DIDN'T COME BACK RIGHT away, I wasn't disappointed exactly, but as my free time in class stretched out past the twenty-minute mark, I knew taking a couple pretty pictures of a tree in the courtyard wouldn't be enough to do well in the class. I had to find out the requirements of the assignment.

Luckily, the Peters were hanging out near the bike racks.

"I took a pretty photo. What else do we need?" I asked.

"You took one photo?" Peter giggled. "We've been out here for twenty minutes."

"There's a whole list. Here."

The other Peter showed me.

There had been a list on the classroom board. A list I hadn't even noticed.

Oh boy.

If I wasn't swept away by the magical High Council soon, my grades would definitely suffer.

"Can I?" I asked.

The other Peter shrugged. "Sure."

"Thanks." I snapped the photo of their photo.

The lighting and quality of the instructions were terrible, but the requirements were all there.

"You're a lifesaver."

"Among other charming things." The Peters laughed.

"There's only one we don't know... specular highlights," Peter pointed out.

"Like a really good hair dye?" the other Peter joked.

"Specular: pertaining to a mirror. Light reflecting on the surface," I parroted the proper definition back to the boys from a place somewhere deep in my memory. "So I guess take a photo of light reflecting off a shiny surface?"

"Whoa. I thought you weren't paying attention." Peter was impressed.

I shrugged.

"I wasn't. My aunt has a big vocabulary."

"And clearly you do too."

The Peters nodded.

"We play Scrabble," I admitted. "Whatever."

"Not whatever. You just turned our A into an A plus," Peter told me.

"One hundred percent," the other Peter agreed.

But then, their focus on school tasks was over.

"So..." Peter raised an eye. "What happened with Spade?"

"False alarm. Everything's fine." I didn't want to talk about it. "I better keep taking these." I nodded to the list.

"Tick, tock. There's only five minutes left," they agreed.

So I strolled away on my own once more.

The teacher had basically created a whole photo list scavenger hunt.

Something beautiful was last on the list.

There were fourteen other pictures to take and only four minutes of free time left. The quality of my work wouldn't be too high if I only had five minutes to fulfill the brief. But I couldn't blame Spade for giving me incomplete info. I should have taken note of the details of the assignment myself. I started checking off the photos one by one: something contrasting, asymmetrical balance, something disproportionate. I took photos big and small.

"What'd you do for forced perspective?" Kate asked when our paths crossed. She was dragging around the guy with whom she'd partnered. I think his name was Martin.

I gave them both a grin.

"I haven't done it yet. Want me to take a picture of you stepping on—sorry, what's your name?" I asked the guy who was her partner.

"Jim," he told me.

Good thing I hadn't called him Martin.

"Yeah, that works great, I—" Kate barreled ahead

"LOOK WHAT I FOUND!" A voice boomed into the courtyard, stopping our discussion in its tracks.

We all turned.

A boy held up an ornate hairbrush. He waved it around, proud as a peacock. For a brief second, I thought it was Spade. Involuntarily, my heart dropped.

"Oh my god!"

But Marcy knew exactly who it was.

Greg jogged towards her, a giant grin on his face.

"You didn't!" Marcy squealed, dropped everything, and ran to him. She threw herself into his arms.

"You did it!"

She began to shower him with kisses.

"WE did it!"

"Oh my god!"

He spun her in the air.

Then shoved his tongue down her throat.

She kissed him back passionately.

While everybody watched.

It felt super gross.

"I love you, babe!"

"I love you more!"

The two really went for it. They didn't care who watched. Maybe even got off on the show. Even from thirty feet away, I could clearly see their tongues as they tilted their heads to and fro. Neither one seemed able to decide which angle was best to stick their tongues down their throats.

"Alright, break it up."

Mr. Hanks pulled the lovebirds apart.

Half-heartedly, he put some distance between the positively glowing teenagers. I wondered if he was aware they'd just received a one-way ticket out of his class.

Probably.

It didn't seem like his first rodeo.

After the initial shock, they regained their composure and kept hands-free, appropriate class distance, but lounged together on the grass, probably picturing their whole lives.

I felt my own hopes and dreams twinge a little.

They seemed so happy.

Could such good news happen to me?

I looked down at my replacement anklet. The beaded bracelet still hung above my foot.

My so-called plan to parabond with myself wasn't working.

"Earth to Mae."

Kate pulled me back from my thoughts. The interruption from her classmates had barely even registered on her face. Jim was also waiting. I brought my attention back to them.

"Right, sorry. Forced perspective."

I brought my digital viewfinder up to eye level.

Kate stood fairly close to me and lifted her right leg and arms in an aggressive position. Her face twisted into a snarl. Jim stood three times the distance away and cowered his body in fear. The result made Kate look like she was a monster stomping on the head of her tiny partner. I snapped several photos in a burst.

"I'll send it to you," I told them, choosing the best one.

"What'd I miss?" Spade suddenly reappeared as I parted from Jim and Kate.

"Uh, how about the whole class?" I complained.

He fell into step beside me.

"Oh, and Greg and Marcy... I think they just parabonded on the lawn."

"When you say it like that, it sounds dirty." He grinned.

"How would you put it?"

"I wouldn't. That word's off limits. Totally hush." Spade gave me a knowing look and I promptly shut my lips.

He was right.

We shouldn't be talking about it.

After all, I didn't want to anger the fates.

It was funny, I was sure I wanted to get into the High Council without him, but the moment I thought Spade was snatched up by someone else, I felt a twinge of something.

Attraction?

Regret?

I liked Spade a little more than I wanted to admit.

I frowned in his direction.

"Let me get a picture of this." He snapped a picture of me.

"Let me guess, that's your something beautiful."

"Nope, it's my something-that-thinks-too-highly-of-itself." He laughed.

I swatted him, aware I was now quick to touch his skin. I pulled my arm back as the happy parabonds passed us by, completely oblivious. He also watched them. After they'd gone, for the first time since I'd known him, Spade gave me what felt like an honest grin. Seeing their successful pairing, there was hope for us yet.

I knew he felt it because I felt it too.

Much as I didn't want to admit it, my interest in Spade was growing.

I gave him a small smile back.

But it wasn't that simple.

My mind hadn't changed. I didn't want to hurt his feelings, especially now that I could see more than just his physical interest, but it was still wrong. It was way too much pressure. Such stress on a newfound partnership shouldn't exist, especially if it was meant to last forever.

Much as my hormones gave off some feel-good little tingles, I knew if the fates wanted me to attend the High Council, it wouldn't be with him.

TWENTY-ONE
NOTHING LIKE THE MOVIES

AFTER THE INITIAL discovery of the bunker with
Aunt Abeline, I spent several afternoons in the secret
basement by myself. I ran my hands over the shabby
wallpapered walls and took the time to dust away the
cobwebs and grime. The rooms quickly came back to
their original glory.

I'd never known my family history.

Before her death, Aunt Abeline and my mom had
been loving sisters, but the women barely talked. I'd
always wondered why, but now I understood.

An entire secret society lived between them.

It was understandable, but the silence meant I
knew very little about my own mom.

Almost nothing, really.

Like the way Aunt Abeline's love of big words had
also found their way into my vocabulary, being
accepted into the High Council would tell me so much
more about who I was and where I came from. It was a

world in which I desperately wanted to immerse myself. After all, I came from a long line of witches, which on its own was a lot to unpack.

I'd never had any secret powers or strange inclinations.

At least, I didn't think I did.

And you would know, wouldn't you?

I sure didn't know any spells.

Aunt Abeline had said being a witch in real life was nothing like in the movies, more like being an athlete than some monster, but if that were true, I had no idea what being a witch really meant. Would I have supernatural powers? Did I have them now? That would be cool. Freaky, but cool. Or maybe it'd be terrible. Maybe becoming a witch would make me an abnormal weirdo. I already felt like an abnormal weirdo sometimes, all on my own.

It wasn't fair.

Sierra would know all these answers. But she was gone.

And there was no one else to talk to.

It's not like I could go running to Josie. She'd made that abundantly clear.

Aunt Abeline was no help. There were only so many times I could look at her sad expression, feel the weight of her own rejection while she pretended to be happy for me, and ask another question that she'd try to help with but to which we both knew she wouldn't know the real answer.

There was someone out there who could answer my questions...

His photo was the one I kept coming back to.

My dad.

He was out there, somewhere.

Once I joined the High Council, maybe I'd meet him?

I wondered if he even knew I existed.

What was their courtship like? Him and Sierra. Did they always know they'd be parabonded together? Or did Grandma Mim and her adult buddies poke and prod and get involved like my aunt and her friends? Did they all celebrate openly and joyfully like I'd seen from Greg and Marcy? Or was it a secret right from the beginning? Could their match have been a total shocking surprise?

Was it too much to hope that they'd loved each other?

At least for some moment?

He looked so nonchalant in the photo. He'd know the answers to all my questions. I wished I could find him.

I pored over the other pictures again and again, looking through the album, checking out the deep background to see if maybe I could catch a glimpse of my dad lurking.

Perhaps he'd been caught on camera candid, unbeknownst to him.

Maybe a photo where he was laughing with another student, or studiously reading a book?

I stared so deeply at each photo that I tired myself out. But I had no luck.

I couldn't find him anywhere.

A couple images had an arm or a leg of a person slightly off camera. Maybe these were him, casually hanging around with my mother's friends. There was no way to know.

As they always did, my eyes came to rest on the last photo in the album. It was a group of six women all posing together, arm in arm. Eternally laughing. My mom had broken the embrace and stretched out towards the camera like she was going to take it away. The other girls were amused, leaning on each other, familiar enough to carry their collective weight.

Girlfriends.

I'd never had that.

Others to help carry the weight.

It was a side effect of so much travel. I never got to know anybody. Not really.

When she'd sat down next to me on the bus, I'd thought for a moment maybe Josie would be someone with whom I could truly connect. I don't know why. It wasn't because Aunt Abeline encouraged me to make friends. It was just a feeling. There was something calming about her energy. But with the parabonding looming over us, she never really gave me a chance. Could I blame her? I was fresh meat in town and a threat to her plan. To her, I might ruin everything.

At least I had Kate. She'd been so welcoming.

I should be nicer to Kate, I thought, yawning.

So she was a little overbearing. Maybe some of the girls in these photos were overbearing too. They could still laugh and have fun together. Maybe the whole point of a group of girlfriends was to overlook each other's little flaws. Kate was a friend every time I needed it. She was helpful and she didn't judge. But you couldn't force friends. Kate couldn't force a connection with me anymore than I could force a connection with Josie.

Josie.

Josie and Beck, a small voice reminded me.

No.

I frowned.

Just Josie.

I'd been staring at the photos for so long, I found it difficult to keep my eyes open. Whirling thoughts of friendship bubbled in my mind as my head lowered, and soon, I drifted off.

The dreamscape that arose was familiar.

I was back on the water, seated in a small boat, paddling. I was above water but dripping wet, soaked to the bone. I reached out for a cloud to dry myself with, its white, airy nature refreshing my skin.

The oar in my hand helped me push through the river.

Faster and faster I went until, as I traveled, there were rapids and white water all around me, and the energy of the water overtook the propulsion of my boat.

Suddenly, the vessel wasn't really a boat at all.

Instead, it was a car on a roller coaster. I held on for deep life as the compartment dipped and folded along a dangerous track. Without actually seeing her, I realized Josie rode in the cart beside me, though we never spoke. On the last hill and valley of the coaster, we drove by a statue, and a swarm of birds was unleashed with great force. I ducked my face to avoid their trajectory, and a cat flopped at my feet offering me his tummy. The bumpy roller coaster ride made no difference to my new furry friend. Softly, he meowed. I reached down to pet his silky coat.

When the ride stopped, Josie left me.

She climbed out of the cart onto a tightrope. Suddenly, she was desperate to flee the scene, but her balance on the thin black rope couldn't hold her. Her hips pitched forward so she arched her back to counter the sway. Her body lurched forward but there was nothing to catch her.

"No!" I screamed as she fell into darkness.

I rushed to the side of the cart to see how she landed.

To hope she was alright.

To make certain of her safety.

But in this dream landscape, imaginary Josie had disappeared forever.

THE REST OF THE WEEK, I searched everywhere I could think of to find my necklace.

I combed the green spaces around the high school and inspected every inch of the walk to and from the school. My anklet wasn't there. The necklace wasn't anywhere.

Josie never sat on the bus with me again, but even from a great distance, I got pretty good at reading the back of her head. She seemed more and more agitated as well. She and Beck had also failed to parabond, I was pretty sure.

My aunt had never really talked aloud about what it felt like to be rejected by the fates, but she did stress that by the time your object was lost, there was already not very much time left.

There were only thirteen days from the new moon to the full one.

Josie and I were on the same limited schedule, and

our expiration dates were about to sour. As the days wore on, my resolve to make it into the High Council on my own also wavered. Being partnered with Spade wouldn't be such a bad thing, would it?

I couldn't really explain my desire to belong to the secret society I knew so little about, but I knew I wanted it.

Mom and Grandma were part of the order, and so was Dad... probably.

If I didn't make it past the initiation, I'd never know more than the whispers of the town. I needed specifics. I wanted to understand who she was. I wanted to see where she'd stood. This was a real chance for me to get to know her better. I wanted it more than I'd ever wanted anything in my whole life.

Since she'd brushed me off on the bus, I'd given Josie nothing but space, but I couldn't shake the feeling that maybe she and I could help each other. Approaching her at school hadn't worked, but there was one place in town where it had. I resolved to see her over the weekend.

When Saturday rolled around, I hopped on my bike and headed back to the mechanic shop. She'd been receptive there once before; hopefully I'd find her in a good mood again.

One-on-one, with no one around, we could speak at length.

Being back on my bike, I felt free.

I remembered riding these same streets at the end of the summers for years, before I'd heard any whispers about some parabonding hocus-pocus. It felt good to pump my legs and feel the wind in my hair.

I made the effort to be present.

The homes of the town's main streets sailed past.

I looked in detail at the little flower boxes and the porch swings, all well hung. Plumpkin was actually a tiny but beautiful place. If I could just figure parabonding out, I was starting to believe I could really make a home here.

I sailed to a stop in front of the barbershop mechanic's.

Again the owner was chatting away, clippers waving about in his hand.

I walked my bike over to the side of the building to the car bays and poked my head in, then stopped in my tracks. Josie's car wasn't up on the blocks. Instead, I could see another kid sitting at a desk stacked with printouts. He hadn't seen me and was totally involved, clicking away on his cell phone. He was somewhat hidden from view behind the pile of tires. I ducked my head back out of view.

It was Beck.

Of course he'd be here.

Josie had said the building belonged to her boyfriend's dad.

Beck was that boyfriend. I should have known.

The way his hand cupped Josie's butt outside in the quad shot through my mind.

She had told me to stay away, but fate kept

bringing him around. It was like I was destined to talk to him.

But that wasn't exactly true.

This wasn't fate.

His presence was a perfectly reasonable result of my visiting his father's shop, which was probably also Beck's home. I just hadn't put that together. And now, I was parsing details that didn't matter.

If Josie wasn't here, there was no point in staying.

I turned to leave, but then stopped.

Unless...

If anyone were to know where to find her, it would be Beck.

I could ask him for help in locating Josie.

No harm in that.

I knew I was way too happy to have found an excuse to open a chat with him.

But I ignored the little voice inside of me that kept repeating this was wrong.

"Hello?" I called out, still perched with one foot on my pedal, one foot on the ground.

He looked up, surprised.

"Mae?" His face lit up in a smile. "Hey. How'd you know where to find me?"

He hopped out of his seat and headed to the front of the bay.

Something told me to keep some distance between us.

"Actually, I was looking for Josie," I admitted,

getting off my bike, kicking the stand out. I stood on one side with him on the other.

"Oh."

Did I register a twinge of disappointment in his expression?

"You and me both." He shrugged, raking a hand through his hair.

I watched his fingers work through the tousled waves just a little too long.

"I have some... questions... for her."

"Shoot," he offered.

I was about to remind him that those questions were for Josie, but I realized maybe this was even better. Beck had been pretty forthcoming before.

"My necklace is still lost," I started.

"I didn't find it... again. Don't worry."

We both grinned.

He took a step closer. Instinctively, I took a step back.

"You and Josie...?"

I enacted a type of bonding with my hands.

He shook his head.

"You and Spade?"

I shook my head no.

"I don't get it. I've looked everywhere," I said.

Beck raised an eyebrow.

"I mean, Spade has," I clarified.

"Yeah. Something's off," he agreed.

Something was off.

Me.

I was off.

Here I was, trying to control my own destiny. Maybe my actions were causing ripples in the fortunes of others. Could I cause unintended consequences for them? Did the flap of a butterfly in Texas cause a storm in New Orleans?

I never told anyone it was my intention to avoid the parabonding couplet but still make it into the High Council selection. But it was possible the fates knew my thoughts.

"My sister... she's there. In the council. She lost her offering and her jock boyfriend found it the same day. I don't think it's supposed to be this hard. By the full moon, they were both gone. That was two years ago, but still..."

"How long has Josie's thing been missing?"

I avoided the word *offering* completely.

"First day of school, same as you."

"Right." I frowned.

"Well, when the time's right, I'm sure you'll find it."

"Glad you have faith," he muttered.

He seemed so sad.

Their inability to parabond was probably causing a lot of stress in their relationship.

"I do," I agreed, looking at him evenly. "I have faith in you."

We gave each other gentle smiles but let the moment pass.

"And I'm sure Spade will find yours."

"Yeah... wait... why? Why him? You said Spade's a turd. You and Josie make a lot of sense. You're boyfriend and girlfriend, you love each other. Why am I matched with Spade? He seems really certain too."

"Spade's mom and your aunt were rejected from the same High Council class."

The late-night phone call. It was a heads-up from an old classmate.

"That's it? They used to be friends and my fate's decided?"

"All our fates are decided." He shrugged.

Beck looked so dejected, I couldn't help but lighten the mood.

"Oh?" I raised an eyebrow. "Was this decided?"

I plunked his hand into a puddle of grease on the table beside him.

"No way." He laughed, pulling his hand back in disbelief.

It dripped with black ooze.

"How about *this*?"

I bopped his hand towards his face, grease plunking a smear from his nose to his cheek.

"Oh no." I giggled. I had never intended my trick to work so well. He looked like a football player who'd gotten a little too eager with the grease paint. "Beck, I'm sorry, I—"

"Oh, you are dead."

"It wasn't me. It was fate!"

"I'll show you what's fate!"

He lunged to catch me, but luckily, I kept the bike between us.

I threw my hands up in defeat.

"I'm sorry. Okay, I'm sorry. Here."

As a peace offering, I dug my own fingers into the grease and dragged black smudges across my cheeks.

"Fate made me a warrior princess." I laughed.

"Warrior genius," Beck agreed.

He took up the art project and dragged more black grease down his own face.

We both grinned.

I wondered if I looked as stupid as he did.

Adrenaline coursed through my veins.

"When I'm parabonded, I'm gonna kick the High Council in the balls!" I shouted.

"When I'm parabonded, I'll karate chop them to the face!" Beck agreed.

"Roundhouse kick to the chest!"

"Karate chop them to the face!"

"You already said that! You've only got one move?"

"Oh, I've got moves…"

For a moment, I thought he was going to try to kiss me.

That's what Spade would have done.

But instead, Beck kicked and karate-chopped in three different directions at once, letting out a tribal yell. His exuberance made me laugh and knocked us both off balance.

"Whoa!"

I reached out my hand, but the tire I used to stop

my tumble started rolling. Beck's large hands grabbed my waist and kept me upright. He swooped me up. But in trying to save me, he left a greasy handprint on my shirt where his hand had held me. He quickly let me go.

"Oh my god, look what you did!"

I swatted him on the chest, leaving a revenge mark of my own.

He yelped just as loudly.

"This is my favorite shirt!" I said.

"This was mine."

"It's just plain gray."

"Plain gray is cute!"

I swatted him again.

Suddenly, we were handsy and messy and laughing maniacally, ruining each other's skin and clothes with more and more stains. Until abruptly, in the entrance of the garage, someone loudly cleared their throat.

Beck and I both froze and turned to see-

"Josie!" I said.

She stared icy daggers.

We straightened up immediately.

"I was looking for you," I added, realizing how feeble that sounded.

I grabbed my shirt, lifted it from the waist, and wiped the grease smears from my face onto the fabric. It was already beyond ruined.

Beck did the same.

With herculean strength, I made no notice of the

peek of abs, the outline of his hips, or the dribble of hair leading down to his jeans.

Josie's dark eyes cut a swath into me.

"We got kinda carried away," Beck started.

"I can explain," I added.

"Save it."

She spun on her heels and got back in her car.

"Josie, wait!" I shouted.

TWENTY-THREE

A REAL CHAMELEON

"COME ON!" I called, already headed for the door.

"Let her go."

Beck tried to grab my hand, but I yanked it away from him.

"You have got to be kidding."

I kicked up the bike stand and turned the bike around to follow her.

"She needs to calm down," Beck called over my shoulder. "She'll only lash out!"

But I sped off in pursuit.

Josie's car was already halfway down the block when I got up and rolling, but she was forced to slow for the red light ahead. I cranked the bike pedals as fast as my legs would take me.

"Pull over!" I called.

The light would change any second.

I sailed to a stop beside her vehicle.

"Josie! It's not what it looked like!"

She refused to look in my direction.

"You're upset. You shouldn't be driving. Let's talk about it!"

In response, Josie revved the engine.

The light turned green, and she blasted away from me. The car behind her waited to see what I would do. I kicked up my feet and pumped the bike in pursuit. It wasn't much of a chase. The other cars in the road politely went around my frantic progression, their engines moving faster than my legs ever could. There was no way to keep up. But when I saw her turn off Main Street onto the lane that the school used as her bus route, I knew where she was going.

Home.

Her stop on the route was only a quarter of a mile or so down the road. If she went there, I could catch up with her once more. I eased up on my pedal speed to a more manageable pace. Thankfully, in such a small town, there wasn't much traffic.

When I got to her street, I made the turn.

Off the main road, the distance between the farmhouses stretched out. The houses were set back from the road and the street was littered with steep valleys and dramatic hills. I was quickly red-faced from the effort.

How could I have flirted with Beck?

How did it get so physical so quickly?

I liked him, and I could tell he liked me too. But what did it matter if he liked me? He loved Josie. And she loved him. I had promised to not get in the middle. I hated when girls got in the middle of things.

But, as I reminded myself, we didn't actually do anything.

Sure, there was a little flirting, and a bit of hands that were a touch too handsy, but we were just joking. Nothing happened. Josie was overreacting.

Still, I had to clear the air.

I should have left when I saw she wasn't in the automotive bays.

I certainly should never have touched him.

I shouldn't have touched anyone.

I could see how it looked, the two of us rolling around in the grease.

It was a bad look.

But that's all it was.

I ignored the little voice inside that wondered if I was rushing so fast to plead my case because I knew deep down, she was right?

No.

We were in this weird paranormal boat together, and I wouldn't make Josie's life any harder than it needed to be. This was just an unhappy accident.

I looked at the various farmhouses. Why hadn't I paid more attention to the stop in front of her house? From my bike on the road, they all looked pretty similar. I remembered the old stump at the base of the driveway. She sat there sometimes as the bus had pulled up. But it turned out lots of these farmhouses had old stumps by the road. If she pulled her car into a garage, I'd have no clue which house was hers.

But I was determined to make things right.

If I had to knock on every door on the street, I would.

Luckily, I didn't have to.

From the road, I spotted her car. She left her old clunker in the driveway.

I brought my bike to a halt at the end of the driveway and looked up at their property.

Josie's house was a beautiful turn of the century farmhouse. The buildings were well cared for. Trees lined both sides of the street. How big her family's land ran was hard to say. A couple of acres for sure.

I hesitated.

Images of farmers with rifles perched on their shoulders protecting their property flashed through my head. What were the real-life rules about trespassing on farm life and what was made up in Hollywood movies? Heading up the unpaved driveway felt a bit risky. I wasn't invited, but it was the only way to talk to the girl.

I was sick and tired.

I didn't ask for any of this.

I didn't ask to move to Plumpkin.

I didn't ask to lose my grandmother's necklace.

I certainly didn't ask to come from a long line of witches...

And neither did Josie.

She was the only one who'd shared anything with

me without some obvious ulterior motives. Sure, she was a bit closed off when she thought I was helpless, but I knew more now. We were equals. And neither of us seemed to be parabonding. If we could help each other, it was worth the risk. I kicked up my foot and peddled up the gravel drive.

As I arrived, Josie's car let out a final sigh from an engine that had been ridden hard.

I thought about what I could possibly say when I got to the front door, but there was no time for prepared speeches. Josie wasn't inside.

She hadn't moved from the driver's seat of her car.

She sat in silence, listening to the hum and hiss of her engine, lost in her own thoughts.

I wheeled my bike beside her car once more, deliberately letting her see and feel my presence before I spoke.

"You're trespassing," she said without making eye contact.

"It's not what it looked like."

"What did it look like?"

This time her dark eyes flashed to mine, daring me to say something she didn't like.

"I went there looking for you."

"You've still got grease on your face."

She let out a sigh and pulled herself out of the car.

I moved aside to give her room and then used my shirt as a face cloth once again.

"Your hands were all over him. His hands—" She couldn't say more.

"It was just joking. Just jokes between friends."

"So now you're friends?"

"No... yes. Sort of?"

I had no clue which answer would please her more.

"I don't know. I was looking for you," I repeated.

"Just leave."

She walked away from me.

"You're the only one I can talk to about this," I tried again.

She spun on her heels to face me, her face seething with anger.

"I don't care, Mae. I don't want to talk to you. I don't want you in my life. I don't want to see your face. I. DON'T. WANT. YOU. Go home."

"You don't understand."

"Oh, I do. I get it. I get you. A real chameleon."

"Thank you?"

"Don't thank me for that. It means you cheat and lie and pretend to fit in with whoever you've got, but no one knows the real you. Ugly little Mae."

"Beck told me that you're having trouble parabonding," I squeaked.

"That's it."

She dug in her pocket.

"I am too! I think there's something happening."

Josie pulled out a small knife. She squeezed a metal button and a blade popped out of its sheath. It flashed in the sunlight. She marched towards me.

"Wait. Omigod. Josie, I'm sorry, I..."

I tried to back up, but the bike and her car were

behind me. I caught my ankle on the tire and both me and the bike fell over.

"No, I'm sorry. Sorry I ever helped you," she said, looming overhead.

Josie raised the knife above her.

I ducked and covered my eyes, as if not seeing the thrust would stop her from inflicting real pain.

Josie swung down and plunged the knife into my tire.

The wheel made an exaggerated hissing sound.

Surprised to be unscathed, I opened my eyes in time to see the wheel lurch when she yanked out the blade.

"There. We're even. Come near me or Beck again and we'll have a serious problem."

Josie stared into my eyes, glowering.

I dropped the gaze, frightened and ashamed.

She was right.

I was trying to force myself on her.

I was no better than someone like Kate.

Her message heard, she turned on her heels, stalked up to the house, and slammed the front door behind her.

For a moment, I sat still.

The shock of violence had rendered me frozen.

I closed my eyes and took a deep breath.

On some level, she was a crazy nut bar.

But on another level, I deserved what I got.

Everything about this was deeply unfair.

I looked down at the tire that Josie had fixed and

now destroyed. It was ripped open with a ragged edge. This time there'd be no hope of repair. I pulled myself to my feet and tested the wheels. I couldn't ride it, but it would still roll.

I started the long walk home.

Why was Josie so stubborn?

If only she'd listened instead of reacting, maybe we'd get to the bottom of this. I could help her. She could help me. I knew she was upset, but stabbing my tire? That was vindictive and weird. I had half a mind to call Beck and show him what his precious girl had done.

The thought brought comfort.

But it was gross.

If I did that, I would be the exact kind of girl she was accusing me of being.

I was better than that.

Plus, I didn't have his number.

The only numbers in my cell were my aunt's and the Peters from graphics class. I wouldn't call any of them to clean up my mess.

As I heard a car approach on the farm road, I pulled my limping bike farther to the side. I didn't turn around, but I heard the car slow.

"Hey there!"

a familiar voice called over the din of their engine.

Kate.

"Need a lift?"

"You're a lifesaver."

I had never been so happy to see her.

"Hop in."

She pulled to a stop and popped her trunk. I dragged my bike to the backseat and lifted it in. Kate got out of the car to help, but I managed all on my own. Her eyebrow raised at the gash in the tire.

"Got a flat?"

"Second time since school started. Can you believe the luck?"

I closed the trunk door, but she still eyed the knife wound through the back window.

"Yeah. That's unlucky."

Next, she eyed my greasy T-shirt, but didn't add anything. I also didn't offer.

We both got in the car, and she set out on the road again.

"Were you out for a ride?" she wondered.

Of course I was out for a ride.

We both knew she was fishing, but since she was helping me out when I so desperately needed it, I decided to satisfy at least some of the questions.

"I had a visit with Josie," I admitted. "It didn't go well."

"Right. I forgot she lives out here."

Kate left it at that.

Josie was wrong, I thought.

I wasn't some chameleon. I didn't lie to Kate. I didn't share all the facts, but so what? Who did?

We drove through Main Street and over the hill to my street. I was about to tell Kate where to turn when I realized her blinker was already on.

"You know where I live?"

"Duh, the school bus drives right by." She shot me a puzzled look.

Of course.

Kate was always on the school bus well before me.

I breathed a sigh of relief.

This whole parabonding nonsense had me tied up in knots. I gave her a tired smile.

"And you have a car?" I noted.

"I told you, I like the bus."

"That's right. You did. You coming along just now was a real lifesaver. If not, I'd be rolling along Route 17 for hours. Guaranteed."

"Happy coincidence. Fate, even."

"Ugh. Don't say that word."

"Happy?"

"Fate. The fates allow. The fates have yet to be kind to me."

"I know what you mean."

Kate nodded.

But I shook my head.

Clearly, she did not.

"Time for a long bath," I murmured as she pulled onto my side street.

Out of the corner of my eye, I detected Kate's face fall just a little. Maybe she'd hoped to keep hanging out with me. Well, tonight was out. After racing across town and being threatened with a knife, I just didn't have the energy. But I vowed to make more time and effort with my one true friend in this town.

"Maybe we can hang out some other day?" I offered.

Kate nodded.

"Actually, a bubble bath sounds pretty good," she agreed. "In my own tub," she added, laughing. "Not to be weird."

"It's heaven."

Kate pulled into my gravel driveway.

"Huh. Looks like heaven will have to wait."

We both looked towards the lake house and the person waiting on my front stoop.

TWENTY-FOUR

WHAT HAPPENED TO YOUR WHEEL?

WHEN THE CAR was in park, I hopped out, my eyes still on my new guest.

Kate came out right behind me.

"What are you doing here?" I asked.

I didn't give him the satisfaction of coming towards him. Instead, I headed to the back of the car to unload the bike. Kate followed.

Spade left the stoop he'd been waiting on to join us. He walked slowly around the car, unsure what to make of my unlikely pairing.

Carefully, I placed my hands on the metal bars to pick up the bike.

He reached in to help.

I could have made a show of how independent I was and gotten the bike out myself, but it was awkward and heavy and I had nothing to prove, so I stepped back.

Spade swooped in and lifted up the frame.

"What happened to your wheel?"

"It's a flat." I shrugged.

Kate said nothing.

He put the bike down at my feet. Next, he looked at my greasy mess of an outfit with a raised eyebrow. Kate didn't have a spot on her. I crossed my arms over my chest but didn't defend myself or explain it. Instead, I waited.

Spade and Kate both forced smiles at one another, but neither spoke or made any motion to leave.

This was going nowhere. I'd have to get the ball rolling.

"Well, thanks again, Kate." I started with my driver.

She seemed surprised, as if she thought it was only natural that she'd get to stay and observe my interaction with Spade. Maybe she'd assumed I wanted back up. She was wrong, but she covered it well.

"Right, no problem. Yeah. You need a lift, Spade? I could drop you somewhere."

Yes, please.

I raised an eyebrow.

Please take him. That would be great.

"I'm good. I wanna chat with mudzilla." He motioned in my direction.

"Right, okay. Great. Well, have a nice weekend." She gave us both a sweet smile. "Enjoy that hot bath," she added.

"I will," I agreed as she got back in her car.

We watched her reverse out of the gravel driveway.

I gave her a weak wave and smiled as she left. We saw her off, but Spade still wasn't talking.

"It's getting late..." I nodded to Spade.

"What really happened?"

His eyes went from my clothes back to the garage where I'd hidden the bike.

The last thing I needed was for Aunt Abeline to worry.

I thought about deflecting, playing the details small, but I couldn't get Josie's words out of my head. Why did I feel the need to prove her wrong? I wasn't a chameleon. I didn't lie to fit in. I would speak my truth.

"Josie happened," I said. "She thought I got too close to her man."

"Did you?"

"Probably," I admitted.

We both took this in.

He took my tone as a positive sign. Clearly, my interaction with Beck had not been a win. Being sort of honest actually felt good.

"It's been a really long day," I reminded him, hoping he'd take the hint.

"I can see that."

He smiled.

I nodded and mustered half a grin.

"I've got something for you," he said.

"Again?"

My energy was so depleted I couldn't summon up

another round of human niceties, but I didn't believe for one second that he was talking about my necklace. That thing was gone. I had searched everywhere for it.

If Spade really had found it, good for him. Our parabond was blessed by fate.

At this point, I didn't even care.

Besides, if it was predetermined, I didn't have a choice.

"Just... humor me."

He led me back to my front porch and bent down where he'd been sitting.

I held my breath and waited for...

Roses?

He picked up a bouquet.

"I came to ask you on a date."

He thrust the flowers towards me.

"A proper date. With flowers and flirting and maybe even a little romance. I like you, Mae. We got off on the wrong foot and that's mostly my fault."

"Mostly?"

I cocked an eyebrow but accepted the flowers.

He grinned.

"Okay, that's totally my fault."

We smiled at each other.

"But I'm not half bad when you get to know me."

I smelled the flowers.

"I think..." he added, maybe not knowing how to quit while he was ahead. I waited for him to make some half-hearted reference to fate and parabonding, but he just grinned.

"I think we'd have fun," he said.

His gentle offer touched something inside.

Maybe that was true.

Maybe we would have fun.

I thought back to Greg and Marcy, the happy couple who'd parabonded and jumped joyfully into each other's arms. Boy/girl relationships didn't have to be so difficult. Spade was handsome. Not in that he's-brooding-and-thoughtful sort of way that Beck exuded, just classically appealing. I definitely found him attractive. Even the first day we met.

Maybe we could fall in love.

The fates would align and we'd make our way up to the High Council.

Okay, I was overthinking things a bit... kind of jumping to the end of the story, but I certainly wasn't making traction on my own. Could we live happily ever after?

One thing was definitely true: if Spade and I became a thing, it would finally put Josie's mind at ease. I'd stop feeling like a desperate home-wrecker and everyone would win.

Not that I'd talk to her again.

I looked up at the kitchen window.

The curtain swayed.

Aunt Abeline had been watching. I thought back to her late-night phone call with Spade's mother. It wasn't just Spade and me involved in this complicated dance. The hopes and dreams of our families were pinned on this too. If we failed, perhaps they failed again.

"What do you say?"

I breathed in the scent of the flowers once more.

"What did you have in mind?"

He broke into a huge grin.

"So, that's a yes?"

I nodded, blushing.

"It's a yes."

"You won't be sorry."

He grabbed me and pulled me in for a hug. He smelled delicious, but I didn't want to appear too eager.

"The flowers!" I laughed.

"Oh, sorry, sorry. Right. Tomorrow night, 7:30."

I nodded.

"Let's synchronize our watches."

"I'm not wearing a watch."

"Sure you are. Let me see your wrist."

He stepped in close. That familiar teasing smile danced on his lips.

I grinned back.

Playing along, I let him compare our imaginary watches on both our empty sleeves.

"A quarter past, good..."

He drew a faint circle on my wrist.

I felt a shiver flow through me.

His smile grew softer, warmer.

"Here, let me see."

I followed his lead and drew a small circle on his wrist as well.

" There. All synchronized."

His energy had changed, grown more still. I could feel the heat from his skin.

"Totally in sync," he agreed, our bodies only inches apart.

"I should... get these in water," I added.

"Sure." He stepped a respectful distance away. "Tomorrow, 7:30."

"Tomorrow," I agreed.

TWENTY-FIVE

ON THE WAY TO SHAKERHEAD LODGE

SPADE WAS BACK at my door the next day at 7:27 p.m.

"I'll just take a picture," Aunt Abeline said. She had been bursting with excitement all day.

"Of our date? That's super weird."

"It's a memento! Of when your love began."

"I barely like him," I objected, but we both knew that wasn't true.

She had caught me sniffing the flowers more than once since last night.

"What? They're nice flowers," I'd objected the first time, but Aunt Abeline's smile said it all. She was on to me.

I just kept replaying that small moment.

His finger circling on my wrist.

He'd stood so close.

He'd stood so still.

"Fine. A secret photo."

"Through the drapes. He'll never know," she agreed. "There he is!"

Aunt Abeline squealed at the sight of Spade pulling into the driveway.

"Oh yeah. Real discreet." I laughed, but also peeked.

Dark jeans, navy sweater, slick brown shoes, and belt with just a touch of white T-shirt underneath. He looked more handsome tonight than I'd ever seen him. The boy cleaned up good, and that effort was all for me. Suddenly, I felt kind of nervous.

"How do I look?" I wondered.

Aunt Abeline dropped the curtain and focused back on me.

"Honey, you look beautiful."

"You're supposed to say that." I frowned. "Oh, my lip gloss!"

I hurried back to the bedroom.

"Smart thinking. Make him wait!" she called after me.

I cringed, hoping her advice hadn't carried through the walls and out to Spade.

My heart was beating quickly.

I dug into the makeup bag on my dresser. The gloss I wanted was an almost translucent shade of pink. I cranked the short wand out of the bottle and slid the shine across my bottom lip.

That was it. That was as good as I was going to get.

I'd said yes to the date as a sort of hypothesis: could Spade and I be happy? Could we parabond together?

But suddenly, it felt very real. I wanted him to like me as much as I liked him. And I really liked him.

I could hear Spade and my aunt on the front porch making small talk. She didn't bother to call back to tell me of his arrival. We all knew he was there. I took one last check in the mirror.

I'd blown out my hair in the morning. It was bouncy and folded around my shoulders in that effortless way that only a lot of effort could create. I wore a black elastic around my wrist as a backup, just in case I needed to pull it out of the way. I doused my lashes in blackest black mascara and used soft pinks and browns to contour my eyes. My cheeks had just a kiss of blush and highlighter. I may never have qualified as some social media model, but I was the very best version of myself tonight.

I glanced down at my dark jeans and white boatneck sweater. The only thing missing was the delicate chain of my grandmother's charm. If things went well tonight, perhaps we'd find it. Spade and I would parabond forever... and ... I shook my head.

Forever could wait.

I opted for cute ankle boots to embrace the fall weather. I assumed we were going to dinner, maybe a movie, but you never knew what Spade had planned.

"Hi." I arrived in the front lobby.

"Hi." Spade gave me an appreciative once over and grinned.

"You two have fun." Aunt Abeline gave a knowing

smile, likely thinking back to her own first date. "Home by eleven," she added.

"Will do," Spade agreed.

"Bye." I smiled.

Out of Spade's eyeline, she waved her camera, ready to take her picture. I rolled my eyes and followed him out the door.

"Here, let me." He opened the car door.

"Thank you." I lowered myself into the car, worried I might hit my own head. This formal date stuff had me a bit on edge.

Spade climbed into the driver's seat.

"Are you ready to be romanced?" His eyes shone.

"Ready," I agreed.

He pulled out of the driveway, and we were on our way.

"So..." I tried to think of something to start the conversation. "Aunt Abeline's weird, right? She wanted to take our picture." I chuckled.

"Oh, I would have posed..." Spade offered.

"Right, for sure." I nodded, changing course.

We drove in silence for a while. Spade concentrated on driving while I looked out the window, trying to maintain my status as an appealing passenger.

"Where are we going?" I wondered.

"It's a surprise." He grinned. "I have a reservation."

"Fancy!"

Then more silence.

"Did you finish your half of the photography assignment?" Spade glanced over at me.

"Oh, yeah. I finished this morning."

"Cool."

"You?"

"Not yet, but I'll get to it."

"Oh yeah, I didn't mean... of course you will. You'll get to it."

The heat between us from last night had disappeared. We both stared out the window. I watched as we drove right through town and kept going. I realized where we must be headed. There was really only one restaurant for miles in this direction that took reservations—the fine dining at Shakerhead Lodge.

"Wanna listen to the radio?" he offered.

"Sure."

He flipped the knob and the car blasted with pop music. He quickly cranked the volume down.

"Sorry, when I'm alone, I guess I listen loud."

"I do that too," I quickly agreed. But my rush to affirm him left us both without a follow up. The pop song filled the void.

Spade drove on into the dark night.

On the farm roads, the municipal government didn't pay for street lighting, so off Main Street, it was just our headlights and the stars to guide our way. We rode on in strained silence. I hadn't been on many dates, but so far I'd say this one wasn't going very well.

"Top forty radio, huh?" I tried again. "I wouldn't have pegged you for a—is that..."

Suddenly, our lights came across a car at the side of the road. Spade and I both looked over.

"Slow down," I told him, but Spade was already slowing.

As we neared, he ventured over the yellow line to give any potential people at the site a little more room. Even in the dark, I recognized the vehicle.

It was Josie's old clunker.

She was sitting in the driver's seat. Her head was tilted back on the seat rest.

"That's Josie," I told him.

Spade swerved off the road and onto the shoulder, stopping maybe twenty feet in front of her car. He threw his vehicle in reverse and drove on the gravel back to her. I looked at Spade with renewed interest as his instinct to help kicked in. A knight in shining armor was appealing. He was busy looking over his shoulder, back to her car. I looked over my shoulder too to see if I could see her or figure out what was wrong.

"She shouldn't be driving such an old car, I told her that," Spade muttered, turning the engine off. "Stay here."

I nodded, watching him hop out of the car and head back to check on his friend. I wasn't scared per se, but I had a pretty good feeling that she wouldn't want to see me. I stayed put in the seat but cranked my body around to watch.

As Spade approached, Josie got out of the car. They stood illuminated in her headlights, talking. She wasn't even happy to see him. The conversation seemed a bit tense... I tried to wait patiently in the car, but soon, I couldn't help myself. I unbuckled my seat belt and got out. Josie had moved to the side, a short distance away, her back to us. She was talking quietly, in the midst of a phone call. I sidled up to Spade.

"Her car broke down and her cell was dead. She was headed to meet Beck for dinner."

"At Shakerhead Lodge?" I wondered.

Spade nodded.

Of course.

In a town this size, there was only one official place for date night.

Or, in their case, an apology dinner.

"She's using my cell to call him."

I nodded. "Okay, I'll just wait in the—"

I started to back away, my curiosity satisfied, but it was too late, Josie was off the call.

She turned and caught sight of me.

"Thanks, Spade."

She handed the phone back without acknowledging my presence.

"Do you wanna ride to the lodge?" he asked.

I nodded, but Josie shook her head.

"We were heading there anyway," I added.

"You knew?" Spade grinned, turning to me.

"I may have figured it out." I returned the smile.

"No, thanks." Josie frowned. "I wouldn't want to ruin your—"

"Date," I finished for her. I slung my arm through Spade's.

She nodded. Finally looking at me.

"Beck's on his way," she said.

"We'll wait with you," Spade offered.

I nodded. No one should be alone on the side of the road without a phone.

"It's fine. He's five minutes away."

"We'll wait," I reassured.

"I don't need your help," she snapped.

She didn't want me there when Beck arrived, I realized. Who could blame her? This was supposed to be the start of their reconciliation. She didn't need the cause of their latest rift still here, still messing about, just waiting to say hello.

"Don't be silly, Jo," Spade objected, but I squeezed his arm.

"It's okay," I told him. "We'll go," I added to her. "But take my phone."

I switched off the lock screen and held it out.

"If you need us, you can call."

I stared her down, my arm outstretched.

If she wanted me gone, she had to borrow my phone. That was the deal.

I wasn't about to leave her on the side of a road, helpless and alone.

She could see I meant business.

"Fine." Josie took the phone from my hand. "Thanks," she murmured.

"Are you sure?" Spade looked between us, bewildered.

"She's sure," I agreed.

"I'm good." Josie nodded. "Enjoy your dinner," she added.

I led Spade back to the car. He still couldn't figure us out, but we buckled back in and pulled out on our way.

"Why didn't you want to stay?" he asked.

"She'll be fine. She's a strong girl. Girl power and all that." I nodded.

We both looked up at the next passing car. Was it Beck, coming to her rescue? Who could say?

"She didn't want me there," I admitted. "She'll be okay."

Spade decided not to push anymore.

We fell into uneasy silence once more until a second set of headlights passed and we both got a good look at the driver. This time it really was Beck on his way to get her. She was right, he had been only moments away. We both sat back in our seats as a feeling of relief set in. I had tried to be tough, but I had been just as worried as Spade. Now that the danger was over, it was time to refocus on us. Spade pulled into the golf course parking lot.

What we needed was a palette cleanser.

"That was pretty attractive," I noted. "The way you knight-in-shining-armored."

"Is that a verb?" Spade teased.

"It is now." I grinned right back. "What time is it?" I wondered.

He glanced at the clock on the dashboard.

"It's cool. We're only a few minutes late."

"No..." I reached out and touched his wrist. "What time is it?"

I made a small circle, then pulled my fingers away.

Warm feelings flooded through me again.

Spade flushed. His smile filled me with hope.

"Oh, let me see," he agreed.

He carefully took my wrist and circled his fingers on my skin.

A spark stirred deep within.

"No, it looks good, seven forty-five."

"Just in time for our reservation," I agreed.

"Just in time." He nodded, his voice smoothing over.

We both smiled at each other.

"Shall we?" he asked.

I nodded.

As we got out of the car, another silence flooded between us. But this quiet was different.

Full of pleasure.

Full of potential.

Brimming with hope.

TWENTY-SIX

A KISS IN THE MOONLIGHT

"WHAT WAS it like growing up in Plumpkin?" I asked, nibbling on a piece of bread from the ornamental basket. The place was even fancier than I'd imagined, with low lighting and cloth tablecloths, but Spade had put his hand on the small of my back as the hostess had led us to our seats, and I didn't care what kind of lighting scheme the restaurant had set up. I was happy to be there.

"Same as growing up anywhere." He shrugged.

"No way." I couldn't help but interrupt. "I've grown up everywhere and Plumpkin is nothing like other towns."

"You mean we're the only place with a pipeline of fate-ties to a secretive underground coven of witches? Shocking."

"Oh wow. So, we're just gonna talk about it?" I leaned in.

Spade shrugged. "You know what I know."

"I doubt that, cuz I know very little."

I had been trying so hard to get information out of Josie, but Spade could be just as reliable. Maybe more so.

"Well, it's all over tomorrow, and this year I hear it's been incredibly thin," he said.

"No, see, I didn't know that. You definitely know more than I do... What do you mean? How thin?"

"At daylight we're donezo. The fates opened the window for two weeks of the moon cycle, the girls lost their... things..."

"Offerings."

"Offerings, right. And the fates chose who'll find them. The traditions travel mostly through family lines. I think this year there are two confirmed parabondings?"

"Greg and Marcy."

"Greg and Marcy and a couple of seniors. Tej and somebody. Have you met him?"

I shook my head no.

"There's others in play like you and Josie. I've never heard of girls losing their things and it taking so long for their stuff to be found."

"Well, maybe for me, it's not fate. Maybe I'm just forgetful."

"Maybe."

Spade looked sad.

"I'm kidding. Sort of. You'll find it."

He offered a smile, but I could see he had been fearing the same thing.

"And once we're parabonded? What then?" I asked.

"I don't know. No one does. No one here, anyway. Once you're accepted, the High Council removes you."

"The fates handpick your spot and you get the hell out of the town?"

"Yup. Some people come back, but no one ever talks about it. Not really."

"Because there are consequences."

I wiggled my fingers like the boogeyman, but Spade didn't grin.

"No joke. When I was seven, this girl at the high school, Evelyn Taggert, bragged to everyone at school that she had enrolled in witch-a-way-camp. She started giving specifics. Two days later, her body was found in the quarry. A drowning accident. That's what they said. Everyone knows it wasn't an accident."

"Could be a coincidence."

"That's not the only sudden death. It's not even the only drowning..."

"So you think this organization is killing people?"

"I think they don't want their actions to be the source of town gossip."

I sat back at the table.

"If it's so dangerous, then how do we know being chosen is even a good thing?"

"We don't. But if you're not chosen, you spend the rest of your life wondering why you weren't good enough." He shrugged.

I could tell he'd seen that.

I guess I had too.

Aunt Abeline's quiet demeanor came to mind. It must be awful to be the one left behind. No wonder she never talked about it.

"This is kinda depressing," I said. "Mind if I change the subject?"

"Shoot."

"Okay..." I tried to think of something, but my mind kept blanking.

"Wanna check the time again?" Spade offered his wrist. His eyes sparkled.

I shoved his limb back across the table.

"You loved it," I told him.

"I did." He grinned. "That's why I'm serious."

He offered it again, wiggling his eyebrows.

Now we were both laughing.

Just then, the server returned with our meals.

"Perfect timing," I deflected, still smiling.

Spade watched the meat and potatoes lowered in front of him.

"It's here when you need it," he mock-whispered, pointing to his wrist as if the server wouldn't hear.

I rolled my eyes, enjoying him.

I had opted for the fancy spinach and pear salad. We both dug into our meals. After the initial rush of delicious tastes and sensations had passed, our conversation continued.

"If ... things... fall through, I'm planning to go out of state," Spade offered. "Better scholarships."

"I doubt my aunt would stay," I agreed. "She writes freelance, so we've always moved around a lot. It wouldn't be hard to leave... I haven't exactly laid down roots."

"What do you mean? You've got Kate and Josie..."

"Josie hates me."

"Fine, you've got Beck," Spade teased, watching my reaction.

I rolled my eyes.

"No, I haven't."

"Okay, but you've got me."

"I do?"

"Hell yeah."

"Thanks."

For a moment, we just smiled at each other. I loved the way he looked out at me from beneath his lowered gaze, as if he were sneaking a peek to see what I thought.

"But you just said you're leaving."

"Maybe you'll give me a reason to stay."

I blushed.

I could think of a few reasons.

After dinner, we still had some time before my curfew, so Spade offered to show me the lookout point on my lake. He was surprised I'd never been to it, and I was surprised to learn it even existed. I was less shocked when we arrived and I realized you had to duck under a chain clearly marked as NO TRES-PASSING to get there.

Aunt Abeline wasn't really the fence hopping type.

Neither was I, but for Spade, I would make the exception.

"This is the Tucker family's land. Their son parabonded fifteen, maybe twenty years ago and they never developed the grounds."

Spade helped me slip under the sign.

"So the locals just help themselves?"

He shrugged. "It's a beautiful property."

The moon was bright, with a huge collection of stars in the clear skies above us. I couldn't see all that well, but I wasn't worried. If we needed flashlights, our cell phones could light the way. Spade offered a hand to help me under the chain, which I readily took. After we'd successfully cleared the sign, he didn't let go. His palm felt warm in mine.

Our pace slowed.

The path weaved through the forest. We were surrounded by trees. I could see the lookout was probably another forty or fifty feet ahead. Spade brought us to a stop in the middle of the overgrown drive. He curved our bodies in to face one another.

"I've had a really nice time tonight," he said.

"Me too," I agreed, feeling the closeness of his breath.

He let go of my hand and raised his fingers to my face. He cupped my neck in his hand and gently pulled me in for a soft, slow kiss. I felt my whole body move towards him in yearning as our lips touched together. His kiss was so soft at first, then opened deeper, more longingly. I followed his passion, matching his rhythms. Before I knew it, I'd slid my tongue into his mouth and his into mine. He tasted sweet, like raspberries picked straight from the vine on a hot July morning. My internal organs vibrated.

"Mmmm."

We murmured together, then pulled apart, breathless.

He looked at me and I smiled back almost shyly. He reached out and touched a stray strand of hair, then grazed my ear as he tucked it behind. My cartilage tingled. It sent a shockwave of desire through my body. His touch was so innocent and so deeply sexual at the same time. I didn't move or blink for fear of breaking the powerful connection between us.

"You're gonna love this," he whispered.

I searched his eyes and suddenly, he took my hand again.

He strode ahead into the woods. I hurried to catch up, willing to follow him anywhere, excited to see where he was taking me. We traipsed down the overgrown path, adrenaline pumping in our ears.

He held back a branch so I could step through and suddenly, we were free of the forest and out on an open rock face clearing that overlooked the whole lake.

"Whoa,"

I said and moved farther into the clearing.

"Just be careful of the edge," he warned.

I looked down. I could see where the rock face dropped off beneath us. But he didn't have to warn me twice. I had no interest in going anywhere near the edge.

"I've been coming here my whole life and I've never seen it from this angle," I marveled.

"Your family's cabin is just over there." He pointed out our small dock on the lake as he came behind me. He slid my hair over one shoulder and gently kissed my neck.

"From here, you'd have a pretty good view. Good to know, as I was skinny-dipping last week," I offered.

Spade raised an eyebrow appreciatively.

"I'd like to see that," he murmured, kissing my neck again.

"Maybe... one day..." I demurred, enjoying each touch. "You're missing the view."

I broke away from his embrace and strolled to the edge of the thicket.

He let me pull away, hopefully relishing the tease of anticipation as much as I was.

After a beat, he casually followed, and when he was close enough, I gave a wicked smile and eagerly pulled him in.

Our lips smashed together more earnestly this time. His mouth was so soft and warm. He applied just enough pressure for me to feel every part of his body. My mouth opened and welcomed his now familiar tongue. I felt his longing.

Deeply.

I know he felt mine.

He smelled like honey and warm apple cider.

My hands caressed his body as his arms encased my shoulders and waist. He wrapped me in towards him. We fumbled, moving back together.

My body pressed into a tree behind us, his warm body in front.

Somehow, Spade instinctually felt this and spun us around so his back was to the bark. His right leg parted mine and we kissed even more deeply, his tongue searching my mouth. His hands started to explore. He pulled me tighter against him, grinding our bodies together. I could feel him more and more. I took his hand and guided it down my hips, reaching for my back pockets like I'd seen Beck do to Josie.

"Oh, yeah," he moaned appreciatively, as I released his fingers to let the grip become his own. He grabbed my butt just like I'd wanted. His hands were forceful and strong against my supple skin. He cupped my cheeks toward him. The angle slid me farther up on him.

Involuntarily, I let out an appreciative groan.

He released his grip then reapplied the pressure, helping my body to rise and rub on him once more.

This was all happening so fast.

I desperately wanted more, but I knew I wasn't ready for it.

The energy and excitement crashed over me, almost more than I could stand, but then his hands floated up near my breasts.

"Take off your top," he whispered, his hand closing

over my breast and nipple through the sweater material.

This was definitely moving too quickly.

I wanted things to slow down but I didn't want to stop.

"Hmm..."

I pretended I didn't hear him, kissing him again.

His fingers trickled down to the hem of the sweater and gently lifted it up.

"Let's take this off," he whispered again.

"What's the rush?" I gave him a little push.

He looked surprised, then pleased.

I closed my lips on him once more.

"You're naughty," he whispered.

Under my sweater, his hands slipped up my back. I knew where they were heading. He wanted to unhook my bra.

"Wait."

I shifted my waist a little to help redirect him.

"Slow down," I murmured breathlessly.

"Why?" He whispered back, kissing my neck and nuzzling my throat.

His lips rose again, and I kissed him deeply.

I wanted him, but not all of him.

Not this minute.

Not tonight.

His hands abandoned their attempts at undressing and found my bottom again. To this, I realized he felt sure, I wouldn't object. His rhythm rock and rolled me, our bodies vibrating together.

But this time, the magic wasn't so potent. I pulled out of the embrace.

"It's only our first date," I told him, coming up for air.

"Oh, you're one of those." He frowned playfully.

It was meant as a tease, but he could see immediately that it was the wrong thing to say.

"And you're one of them?" I agreed, frowning for real.

"I was just kidding, come on. Come here."

He tried to regain the momentum, but I put my hands on his shoulders.

"It's almost curfew. We should get going."

I physically extricated myself from his warmth, shivering as I went.

"We have time," he offered, but we both knew the moment was over.

"I think we should go," I said, heading towards the clearing.

But Spade didn't follow.

"Well, I think we should have sex."

"Now it's *really* time to go." I dropped any pretense.

"You told the Peters that you wanted a relationship with your parabond."

"You were listening to our conversation? That's why you asked me on a date?"

"Don't look so shocked. I like you, Mae, but there isn't time to dick around. Tonight's our last shot. We have to show the universe that we're compatible. Let's pound it out!"

"Do you even hear yourself? Let's go."

"You like me, you obviously like this." He waved a hand over his body. "What's the problem?"

Hearing him describe my sexual appetite in such a crass way felt dirty. I had half a mind to tell him the reason I'd manipulated the way that he'd touched me and who he was emulating when he grabbed my butt.

But that would be ludicrous.

This topic wasn't up for discussion.

I marched back up the gravel walkway, smacking tree branches out of my way as I went.

"Take me home, Spade."

"Fine. Geez. Get in," he grumbled and followed.

I opened my own car door and he drove me back to my house.

"You're making a mistake," he said in the driveway.

"Actually, I just corrected it," I told him, climbing out of the car.

I was about to slam the door when he leaned over.

"You owe me twenty-six dollars for dinner," he told me.

"And to think, we could have been bonded for life."

I slammed the car door.

TWENTY-SEVEN

WASH YOUR TROUBLES AWAY

SPADE SQUEALED out of the driveway.

I wished we had been a bit quieter with my home-coming; I didn't want my aunt to know what had tran-spired. But it was too late. When I looked up at the kitchen curtains, they were already on the move. She knew I was home, and she knew I wasn't happy.

Still, I couldn't bring myself to go inside.

If I went in, she'd have to ask what happened.

It was a stupid conversation to have because anyone with a brain could see that our night didn't go well. Who wanted to talk about how their dream date just imploded?

I sunk down on the front steps.

Aunt Abeline left me to stew in my own juices for a while, but when I still didn't come in the house after twenty minutes, she finally came out on the stoop.

"So?"

"I didn't parabond," I said flatly.

She nodded and we both sat quietly for a while.

"Do you want to talk about it?" she asked finally.

"I really don't."

"Okay."

We slipped back into silence.

Don't tell me it'll be okay, I silently vented, turning the anger I'd felt towards myself and Spade onto an imaginary conversation with my aunt. You don't understand. Adults think they do, but they're always wrong. Your thing is not my thing. Just leave me alone.

I stared hard at the gravel driveway.

You don't know and neither does Josie.

So what if I was a chameleon? I fumed to myself. I tried to be honest with Spade and look what I got. A steaming pile of nothing.

Aunt Abeline didn't push. She took a deep breath and let out a sigh.

"I'm off to bed," was all she said. "Oh, and it's your turn."

I nodded.

But luckily, she knew this wasn't the right time to discuss her latest Scrabble word.

I should just go to bed too, I thought.

No point in staying up.

It was over.

My hopes for the High Council were ruined.

Soon, this would be just another thing we didn't talk about.

"Come in when you're ready."

I didn't look up as she left. I didn't do much of

anything. I just sat on the hard step at the front of the house for a while longer, staring up at the trees. I stayed in that spot until my bones and joints grew cold.

My posture stiffened and sitting where I was became unpleasant, but I still wasn't ready to go back inside.

Instead, I walked down to the water.

So this was it.

Tonight was the end of the fortnight and I had officially failed.

It was bittersweet.

Honestly, I was relieved.

Learning about this strange, mythical society that I was supposed to be some secret member of had brought me nothing but anguish. I was glad that was over.

But I was also sad.

Now with its passing, I was free of its burden. But the chance to really get to know my family had also disappeared. Grandma Mim and Mom were gone, and I'd forever joined Aunt Abeline on the outside looking in.

The rush of the secret world had lured me, lulled me into a desire for some type of safety or precious belonging that simply wasn't real. Instead, I'd found Spade's manipulation. I couldn't believe I'd found that jerk so attractive. I'd come dangerously close to fully letting him in.

What was I thinking?

I needed was to wash away all this karma that had been following me around since the school year began.

I touched my booted toe to the water and watch the ripples the small impression created.

That skinny-dip on the first day of school had been so freeing.

I needed to lighten the weight of the last few days.

The water did look inviting.

My eyes drifted across to the cliff that I now knew as Tucker's lookout. I wasn't afraid of being spotted. After tonight's disastrous date, that was the last place Spade might return. Besides, our dock was only a small dot on the lake's landscape.

Could I do it?

Go fully naked again?

The air was cooler tonight than it had been then, but the symbolism was appealing.

Why not? I thought. I could even tell my aunt I was doing it. I couldn't care less.

I yanked the white sweater I'd so lovingly chosen for my date over my head and threw it in a heap on the chair. I would never wear that tainted top again, forever stained with the memory of Spade's rummaging hands. My skin rippled with goose bumps as I stood in my bra.

I felt good about my choice.

This was my skin and my body.

Spade didn't get a say.

I was in control of who and what would caress it.

Next, I pulled off the ankle boots and tiny socks.

Finally, I dropped my jeans. These I carefully folded. I could have been just as symbolically disgusted with my pants as I was with my shirt, but jeans that fit well and looked cute were hard to come by, so I was happy to leave them be and let the sweater take on all my pathos.

The night was colder than I'd first thought.

I stood on the shore in a bra and undies, letting my skin acclimatize to the cold. It wasn't too late to back out of the skinny-dip, but the idea of stripping free was enticing, even if I just ran in and right back out.

It was a statement.

It was a message.

I snapped off my bra and slipped my panties to the floor.

The fact that I was happy to give myself to the lagoon, to open my inhibitions and my own desires in ways I refused to give to Spade, felt so pure.

I walked into the water and dove beneath the surface.

My hours of primping and priming my hair and makeup were undone in an instant.

It felt good to be free. I was once more just plain old me.

Free of the town's expectations.

Free of the High Council and parabonding.

Free of the shackles of a future already decided.

Free of my family.

That last one hurt a little. The little knowledge I had of my mom and dad was likely all I would ever learn. But they were never fully out of reach. I still had the photographs of my parents. I had my mom's old journals. I'd seen the secret places she dwelled. Perhaps that was all the information I would ever have. But it was all I'd ever need.

Now that I too had been rejected, maybe Aunt Abeline would open up and tell me more about her life on the outside looking in. Or maybe she wouldn't. Either way, we'd both still love each other. Even in silence, we'd both survive.

We could put this small town and the lake house in our rear view.

I wouldn't mind if she sold the family home completely. This old place with so many secrets, so many unanswered questions. It was time to focus on the future. Find somewhere new to make fresh memories.

I tipped myself back in the water to stare at the sky.

It was actually warmer in the lake than in the night air. Taking this dip was really clearing the fog.

The water lapped around me, framing my face, floating my tresses into a beautiful halo. I kept my ears submerged and listened to the moans and groans of marine life. It was quieter than two weeks ago, but just as full of promise and safety and calm. I willed myself to stay in the liquid embrace just a bit longer.

Hold on to this moment.

Hold on.

And then it was over.

I kicked my feet down and felt my toes on the sand. On the shoreline, I heard the familiar snap of branches from my new woodland comrade.

I offered a *tut-tut* rebuke.

But when I looked to the shore, I didn't see an adorable creature.

Standing beside my folded clothes and discarded underthings wasn't a furry friend.

It wasn't a friend at all.

It was Josie.

TWENTY-EIGHT
WE'RE NOT ALONE

"I CAME TO RETURN YOUR PHONE," she said. "I heard you splashing. I didn't know you were... alone."

Awkwardly, she dropped the device with my belongings on the chair.

"Thanks."

I was grateful she didn't choose to point out my lack of clothing. Underwater, I stepped farther back down the natural slope of the beach, further covering my nakedness up to my neck.

"Beck told me nothing happened," she added.

"And you believe him?"

She shrugged.

But I could tell that she did.

"He says it's not fair I'm taking my frustrations out on you."

"I can take it."

Josie nodded.

"I'll get you another wheel," she said.

She paused a moment more, then nodded. She seemed ready to leave but stopped.

"Is this... what you thought life would be like when you decided to move here?"

"I didn't decide."

I shook my head.

"I was told. Nobody asked if this was something I wanted."

"Yeah, well, me neither."

"I'm getting cold. Would you toss me my sweater?"

"It'll get soaked..."

She seemed unsure.

"It's either wet or naked. Pick your poison. Undies too?"

She tossed me the sweater. It splashed in the shallows, but I was able to grab it easily. Then she flung my panties in my general direction. I yanked the sweater over my head and let it float in the waters around me slowly, taking on more and more water. The fabric distorted and pulled. Below the surface, I tugged the ballooning undies around my private areas once more. Josie couldn't help but watch my antics.

"You don't seem like the type," she commented.

"To what?"

"Skinny-dip."

In their waterlogged condition, the fabrics sagged as I moved to the shore. I clamped them tighter around my body.

"I've already been called a prude once tonight.

Let's not pretend we know anything about each other."

"Fine."

"You don't know me," I told her. "You never even tried."

"Well, what did you want, Mae? To sit around and sing campfire songs? Maybe spill secrets while we braid each other's hair? I'm not like that."

"I'm not either. I just thought we could help each other."

"How could you help me?" She guffawed.

But I was out of patience.

"I don't know, Josie. We could have talked about it. Shared our thoughts, compared notes. We could have been civil about things. Instead, you stabbed me in the bike!" It came out as a shout. Until now, I had walked on eggshells in an attempt to please her, but my days of coddling her feelings were over.

The whole thing was so ridiculous. Me, matted down like a wet dog, yelling at her on the shore.

It seemed absurd.

She started giggling, then full out laughing.

I couldn't help it. In spite of myself, I laughed too.

We cackled together.

"There she is. Ugly Little Mae. Just my type," Josie noted.

"Oh, yeah. We make a fine pair," I said. But I smiled.

Josie did too.

Suddenly, the cold war was over.

I regarded her closely.

"It turns out my house has a secret bunker," I offered.

"My house has a false basement," Josie agreed.

Secret rooms, it seemed, were a must in the High Council.

We really should compare notes.

I eyed her, wary, but decided to go for it.

What the hell.

"You wanna see it?"

"If you put on some clothes," Josie agreed.

"What, you don't like my outfit?" I asked, dusting the sand off my feet before putting back on my ankle boots.

"Oh yeah, let me get a picture for the yearbook."

Josie pulled out her cell phone.

"You wouldn't."

"Say cheese!" she joked.

Josie pretended to take a photo.

"Don't you dare!"

I lunged to stop her.

She squirmed, keeping her phone at an arm's length from me.

"I thought your battery was broken!" I complained.

"It was dead, but it's fully charged now. Ah, you're wet. Okay, stop!"

"Put it away. Put it back in your pocket!"

"Okay, okay! It's gone. I put it away."

She showed both her hands to prove the offending camera was hidden.

"You walk in front," I commanded.

There was no way I'd risk a pic of my soggy, sagging bottom.

"My aunt's already gone to bed for the night, so when we go in, tread lightly,"

I warned as we approached the cottage door.

We tiptoed inside and left our shoes at the door.

Josie eyed our Scrabble game with interest but said nothing.

I showed her into the guest room and held up my index finger, indicating to wait a moment until I returned. Josie sat on the edge of the bed.

It only took a moment to duck into my bedroom, strip off the wet clothes, and put on something comfy and warm.

Josie politely waited.

After I'd laid my sodden mess out on the deck railing, I showed her the secret opening that was waiting just below the floor.

"Come on," I said.

We descended together.

Josie touched the walls and opened all the doors just as I had on my first visit.

Finally, we sat together at the table and looked through the old photo album. When we flipped to the final page, the one with the group of women, Josie sucked in air.

"I think that's my mom," she said, pointing to a different woman in the photo.

"My mom too."

I pointed her out.

"I guess they were friends," she said.

"I guess they were."

Josie stared at it for a moment.

I couldn't tell what she was thinking, but I understood how she must've felt. Catching a glimpse of your parents in such a casual, unscripted moment and getting a sense of who they were when they were young was a rare treat. A private smile danced on her lips, but then she caught herself.

"Do you mind if I take a photo of your photo?" she asked.

"Sure."

I looked closer at the girls in the picture. Usually, I focused on Sierra and tried to get in her headspace and feel what she was feeling. But this time, I looked closer at Josie's mom. She looked really happy to be part of the clan.

Josie took out her cell phone and framed her picture of my picture. She captured it on her phone.

I then looked at the rest of the picture.

I hadn't paid any attention before, but there was something a little fuzzy in the background. I wondered what it was. If I unfocused my eyes, the background of the picture started to look a bit clearer. I relaxed my vision, trying to let my peripheral vision build it more clearly. Something about the fuzzy blob in the background behind the girls seemed so familiar.

"Look at that."

I pointed to the blur in the picture. Maybe Josie could make it out.

"Holy, crap. It's Kate."

I looked even closer.

"What? That's impossible."

But she was right, it did sort of look like...

"Not there, here!"

Josie handed me her cell phone.

"Look."

Her digital camera roll was open to the picture of my picture. I thought she would zoom in, but instead, she swiped backwards to the previous photo. There was an accidental picture she'd taken in our play fight at the lake. My blurry butt took up most of the screen. The shock of white from my stretched-out sweater brightly contrasted with the darkness of the forest.

"Omigod, delete that photo! Delete. Delete!"

"I will," she agreed. "I didn't mean to take it, but look."

She zoomed in on the woods behind my shoulder.

Hidden in the darkness was a figure.

"What is that?"

"Not what, *who*."

She zoomed again.

"No way... you're right. It looks like... Kate?" I agreed. "She was hiding in the bushes?"

Our eyes grew wide as saucers.

"That girl is beyond weird," Josie said.

She shook her head, then flipped back to the photo of our parents.

It was more than *weird*.

It was scary.

What was Kate doing here?

Why was she hiding in the darkness?

What had she hoped to see?

Was she there when I'd been skinny-dipping? That was creepy enough, but the more I thought about it, the creepier things seemed. She was everywhere I went. I thought about all the times she popped up in my life: on the bus, in my class, around the town. I had taken her demeanor as friendly, but now that I thought about it, she showed up almost everywhere I went. I had brushed it off as part of life in a small town, but there was no one else I ran into nearly as frequently. And now this? Skulking in my backyard forest in the middle of the night?

There was no explanation for this.

Josie went back to the photo of our moms. Looking in the phone's powerful viewfinder, it was easier to zoom in on the old photo too.

"And look."

I grabbed Josie's arm.

"Ow, what?"

"Zoom in over your mom's shoulder."

She followed my command.

"She's there too," I said.

I slid the picture so her mom wasn't in the center frame.

"Holy crap balls. It's Kate."

"It looks just like her."

"How is she...?"

"This picture is from like twenty years ago. Do you think it's her mom?" I asked.

"I... don't know what to think."

Suddenly, the floorboards creaked above us.

Josie and I stared up at the ceiling, then looked back between us.

Horrified, neither of us had to say it. We both immediately had the same thought.

Kate!

TWENTY-NINE
FLICKERING LIGHTS FROM ABOVE

JOSIE and I fled out of the basement, through the lake house, and out into my front yard. On our way, I turned on every exterior light that we owned.

"Kate?!"

We called out into the darkness.

"We know you're out here." Josie said.

"Come talk to us." I added. "Kate?!"

The lightbulbs from the front and side porch cast deep shadows into the forest, but no one came forward.

"Come on."

Josie lunged into the darkness without fear.

I followed, but I didn't know if I wanted to find her.

What was I hoping for?

Kate was hanging out in the bushes, just watching?

That was seriously creepy. There was no explanation that would make that behavior okay.

But I also didn't want the surveillance to continue.

At least if we confronted her tonight, I had Josie by my side.

"Kate?"

"She's not here," Josie admitted.

"Then we go to her," I suggested. I was surprised by my own bravado. "Do you know where she lives?"

"Yeah, I know it. Come on."

I had the presence of mind to turn off most of the lights. I didn't want my aunt to awaken in the middle of the night and be blinded by what she saw. It was a stroke of luck we hadn't already woken her up.

We took Josie's car. Two women on a mission. Neither of us spoke.

How many summers had Aunt Abeline and I rolled into Plumpkin for a breezy long weekend, looking out the windows, enjoying the peace and quiet of a quaint, friendly town?

Tonight, the streets didn't feel as charming.

In moments, we were off Main Street and out into farmland. Josie drove so fast on the hills that the road began to feel like a roller coaster. Up and down our little car flew. Whatever had been wrong with the engine earlier tonight was totally repaired now. I opened a window and gulped in fresh air.

What would we say if and when we found her?

It was well after midnight, not exactly the time for a friendly hello.

"Maybe we should report it..." I suggested, although I wasn't sure what good that would do.

Kate was sure to know her behavior was wrong.

"To who, the High Council?"

I nodded.

Josie shook her head.

"They reach out to you, not the other way around."

"We could go to the police."

"So they can tell her that spying on other people is gross?"

"They could arrest her for peeping."

"I think she's done more than that."

The second Josie said it, I felt it too.

Kate had messed with our offerings. I hadn't messed things up. Somehow, *she* had stopped our parabonding. She was spying to make sure her little strategy worked.

"She screwed up the reaping," I said out loud.

Josie nodded.

"Well, maybe that was part of it. Maybe fate knew she would mess with things and the universe did it on purpose. Maybe fate doesn't want to tie us to a couple bozos," I said.

"Beck's not a bozo."

"Well, Spade is."

We both darkly chuckled at the statement that was as sad as it was true.

Clearly, Josie had the same opinion I did from her own experiences with him too.

"Maybe you're right," she reflected. "I guess we'll see. That's her house."

Josie motioned to the coming residence, slowing down.

Up a steep gravel road was another set of turn of the century buildings. The long, unpaved driveway made it hard to see the framework of structures from the road. There was the main house, a large barn and a small one, and standing on its own, a grain silo.

The home was darkened.

The closed windows were all dressed with shutters that hadn't seen fresh paint in years. They creaked in the wind. There was no car in the driveway and no exterior light.

"Looks like nobody's home," I said, feeling sort of relieved.

"That just means she's parked near the barn," Josie told me.

She cranked her car to a stop on the side of the road and got out.

"What are you doing?" I followed. "Where are you going?"

My voice grew more panicked as I recognized her intentions.

"I'm going to confront her."

"What? No."

"Yeah."

"Well, at least pull into the driveway."

"And announce that we're here? You kind of suck at this."

"I'm sorry I don't have much practice confronting stalkers in the middle of the night."

"We creep up on her like she was creepin' on us," Josie said.

There was no more discussion.

She left her car and headed up the dirt road at a quick pace. She kept herself low and close to the cover of the ditch culvert at the side of the road.

"What are you gonna do when we find her?" I asked, desperately following.

I thought about the pocketknife she'd thrust into my tire.

Josie was a bit of a loose cannon.

She marched quickly ahead.

"Wait up," I said.

If she flew off the handle with Kate, maybe I could cool things down.

We moved up the property towards the farmhouse.

Kate's home was overgrown and red brick with beige accents around the windows. The panes were very small, likely part of the original build. They offered the homeowners a lot of light but little view. I wondered if inside, anyone stood at those small windows, watching us as we approached. Built around the house was a wraparound deck with two rocking chairs and a porch swing. Everything inside the four walls was pitch black. No sign of anyone moving. But that was to be expected in the middle of the night. The lawns hadn't seen a mowing in many weeks. Maybe even the whole summer. The buildings felt lived in, but not cared for.

"Come on."

Josie led the way, moving around the side of the farmhouse.

The exterior facing away from the road was even more beat up and overgrown than the sides had been. From here, we had sight of the rest of her property.

Josie was right.

Kate's car was parked beside the larger of the two old barns. The old walls soared three or four stories in the air. A light flickered on and off in the hayloft.

"There you are," Josie whispered.

"What's our plan?" I asked, trying to slow things down, but the issue wasn't up for discussion.

"We go see Kate."

I looked up at the flickering light in the barn that awaited us.

"And?"

"And we'll figure out the rest when we get there," she said, moving with intention.

"That's what I'm afraid of," I said to no one in particular, then followed her on.

THIRTY

UP THE LADDER

ALTHOUGH I HAD DRIVEN by many barns in my life, this was the first one I experienced up close.

The bottom layer of the building was built into the hillside. The wall rising from the ground was formed by a mixture of stone and concrete, creating an impenetrable foundation. Above the rock base, the facade was built out of large slats of barn board that had long since grown weathered. The structure looked ancient and haggard, but also strong and proud. It wasn't insulated or airtight like the walls of a house, and through the cracks in the boards, it was clear a man-made light source emanated from inside, up a higher level, deep inside the barn. The gaps and knots in the walls offered small glimpses into the structure's insides. I could see the ground floor was mostly open. There were several pieces of old machinery that had at one time been used in heavy rotation. One day, they had been backed onto the barn floor and then never moved again. Dust and hay were strewn across the flooring. No one had swept out this building in years. It also looked like the spaces might have once been filled with animals, but now the stalls were broken and settled in disrepair. We traveled around the length of the building until we came to the double barn doors. One was left ajar.

From our new vantage point, we could see the flickering light we'd seen from the outside was a candle, although the gleam of the flame seemed unusually bright. It bathed the soaring hayloft above us in a range of golden tones.

Upstairs, we could hear Kate's voice whispering a strange incantation.

Josie put a finger to her lips and pointed up to the loft. After that, she pointed to the barn's built-in ladder. Quickly, she motioned she was going up.

"No," I whispered back.

"I'm going," Josie returned my whisper. "Stay here if you like."

Somehow, waiting alone outside a darkened property with creepy old farm equipment while candles burned and ritualized moaning floated down from the floor above me seemed like a much worse alternative than whatever Josie had in mind.

I'd come this far.

Reluctantly, I followed her in.

Our shoes barely made a noise as we crossed the concrete threshold.

Although the space inside the barn was large, I

couldn't help but huddle, trying to take up as little space as possible.

Josie pointed up the rustic three-person-wide ladder that opened to the outside edge of the loft. The steps had been built when the barn was raised, and their beams were strong and tall.

I tried to grab her shoulder.

I thought we should stop.

Think a little.

Talk about it.

But Josie had already started climbing.

I moved beside her on the ladder and followed her up. When I managed to align myself on Josie's level, almost a story in the air, I tried again to get her attention.

"We should go," I hissed to Josie.

She ignored me.

Suddenly, Kate's face appeared over the ledge of the upper decking. Her eyes were wild, and her skin glowed in the candlelight.

"No," Kate told us, her voice eerily calm. "You should stay."

THIRTY-ONE

HOME OF THE HIGH, MOST HOLY COUNCIL

"WELCOME TO MY HAYLOFT, home of the High, Most Holy Council. I've been expecting you."

Kate stepped back from the ledge to let us join her on the loft level.

Both Josie and I climbed up to reach the top level of the barn.

The loft level covered only half the barn's floor space below, opening to ground level with a dramatic drop-off ledge.

There was no safety railing.

"High, Most Holy Council? Is that the full name of the High Council?" I wondered.

"No," Josie said. "This isn't good."

We took in our surroundings.

The warm glow we'd seen from below wasn't from one candle. There were actually forty or fifty waxen flames lit all around the loft. While it was both eerie and quite beautiful, I couldn't help but feel the ambiance was a pretty serious fire hazard.

Nothing about this attic felt safe.

"What is all this?" Josie questioned Kate.

"I told you. It's the meeting place of the High, Most Holy Council."

"It looks like the set of a high school production of *The Crucible*. Where are the lights?"

"There's no power. Only these."

She waved to her candles.

Josie looked at me and rolled her eyes.

"Are you serious, there's no safer light source?"

"The barn was built in, like, the 1800s. What do you want from me?" Kate shrugged. "You two are late. We're starting our own witches council, since none of us parabonded." She put back on her creepy, ethereal vibe.

"How do you know we didn't parabond?" Josie asked.

Kate smiled.

"You're here, aren't you?"

"You did it. You messed with our offerings," I said. I looked around, half expecting to see them here, built up in a weird shrine.

"Fate intervened. Don't you see? This is exactly what the universe planned."

"What do you think of the universe's plan, Mae?" Josie asked with a frown.

"I'm not exactly pleased," I hedged.

"Oh no. She's loon-toon crazy. Tell her what you

really think. You're cuckoo for Kate-kate," Josie taunted her, but the girl barely blinked.

"Being mean isn't helping," I warned.

"Whatever. Look around. If we can find them, maybe it's not too late," Josie said.

"Kate? Where'd you put them?" I prodded.

"What?"

"Our stuff."

"The universe provides." Kate shrugged. "The earth mother takes away."

"Cut the crap, what'd you do with them?" Josie was done making nice.

"Okay, geez, don't yell."

Kate dropped her gossamer projection and came back to her plain old self. "Yeah, fine. I took 'em. At first, I thought you and I would be parabonded." She motioned to me.

I shivered at the thought.

"But then, I found yours too." She nodded at Josie. "And that's when I realized what the universe really wanted... for the three of us to form our own unbeatable coven. A sister society without the trappings of men. The High, Most Holy Council."

"So you befriended us and stole our most precious belongings without even a discussion. Then you hid in the bushes to see what happened?" I asked. "Why didn't you knock on the door?"

"Oh, I knocked, Mae. I've been knocking. Every time I get close to you, you turn the other way... I saw you at the bank, you know. I know you saw me."

She was wrong.

I hadn't seen her at the bank.

I'd barely noticed her at school.

But she was right too.

I thought back to all her needy attempts at friendship.

I always rebuffed her tagging along. It all seemed so desperate. But I never told her how I felt. Not really. If she had knocked metaphorically, or even physically... I wouldn't have answered.

"So fate intervened," I said.

She shrugged happily.

"Start looking for your offering," Josie instructed, almost knocking over a group of candles in her stead.

"Fine," I agreed, also now looking. "But be careful."

"Look all you want, those things are free as the birds."

Kate dramatically thrust her arms into the air. Suddenly, I imagined a flock of birds swooping out of her arms. Instinctively, I ducked and shielded my face.

A rush of déjà vu hit me.

That was an image I had already seen.

But where?

Ohhh... it was just like my dream. The reoccurring one. This was all like in my dream... a pool of water, a roller coaster ride led by Josie's manic driving, and now the imagery of a dramatic release of birds—I had seen this all before.

But what came next?

I tried to recall more of the dreamscape.

Josie tore apart the loft, looking in every corner as Kate happily hummed to herself. She ignored all our social cues of discomfort. Instead, she drew a circle on the floor.

There was something about a cat looking for comfort.

"Josie, is your offering catlike?"

"You found it?"

"No, I—"

"She just knows!"

Kate clapped her hands together, so pleased. "

She knows everything. See, I told you, the fates brought us here. They bind us together in love and in blood."

Her eyes had taken on an otherworldly sheen.

"I think we should leave. I think we should go. We should get the hell out of here," I spoke to Josie in slow and calm tones so as not to disturb Kate, as though she might not hear me if I spoke at a timbre low enough, although she was only three feet from where I stood.

"How did you know my charm was feline?" Josie asked.

As I looked in her eyes in the candlelight, I could see she'd gone a little wild as well.

"I had a dream..." I admitted. "Why don't we come back and look in the morning?"

"You know why."

The deadline for the High Council would arrive with first light.

"Mae, if you dreamed this, then Kate is right. Fate

did show up. It's intervening even now. The dream will show you how we get out of this. What happened next?"

"We all went home and had a good sleep."

"What happened!?"

"I don't want to—"

"What happened?!"

"YOU WALKED A TIGHTROPE AND FELL TO YOUR DEATH!" I didn't remember it, so much as a regurgitated memory came tumbling out.

"Okay," Josie tried to calm me down. She got real quiet and looked around. "Where's the rope?"

"Are you crazy? You're not doing that."

"She is." Kate giggled, rocking back and forth. "She's totally mad."

She sat at the edge of the circle she'd drawn, watching us like a kid watched Saturday morning cartoons.

"Isn't this great?" Kate grinned.

"Here." Josie found an old rope. "Tie this."

She forced it around an old beam and started tying it.

"I'll walk across." She said.

"It's not—" I tried to object.

"I'LL DO IT!"

"Whee!" Kate laughed and clapped.

"I don't think it's literal! In my dream, the roller coaster—that was you driving, and the birds, they came when Kate raised her arms."

"Then what?"

"The rope might not be a rope," I finished.

And the death might not mean she'd die? I hoped.

We looked around.

"The black line on the floor!"

Josie ran over and began walking the drawing that Kate had made on the floor.

She had to step over Kate, but nothing happened.

Somehow, I knew in my bones that wasn't correct.

I looked past her.

It was something bigger.

I felt it.

My eyes traveled around the barn away from the loft platform.

There were beams in the ceiling leading across the whole roofline. They ended at the rooster's perch.

I squinted.

Did I see a small sparkle in the hay on the other side of the barn?

I shook my head; it was only in my mind.

"Why aren't you watching, Mae? Josie is saving the world!" Kate taunted.

I squinted and looked harder.

If Kate was trying to pull away my attention, maybe there was something there after all? I picked up a candle and swayed the flame left and right, looking for another reflection.

There it was again.

A glint of light.

There was something shiny in the rooster perch on the other side of the building.

"This isn't working." Josie gave up.

"I don't think that's the tightrope," I realized.

I put my hand on one of the narrow, hundred-year-old beams that traveled the length of the barn, three stories above the ground.

"This is."

THIRTY-TWO

WALK THE TIGHTROPE

"LOOK."

I pointed to the rooster nest, but before I could show her the reflection, Kate blew out the candle I was holding in my hand. It let out a dramatic tuft of smoke.

"I don't see anything,"

Josie said, squinting.

I picked up another candle and waved it in several directions, trying to catch the light again, but she was right.

The reflection was gone.

"You saw it?"

Josie turned to me. Her eyes were wild and searching.

"I did."

"Then I'll go."

"You can't walk the tightrope. If you do, you'll fall," I said.

"You said yourself, it's not always literal. Maybe

the fall doesn't mean fall. Maybe it means something else."

"And to check the hypothesis, we should test with your life? It's not worth the risk."

I put my hand on her shoulder, but Josie wrenched away.

"It is worth it! Mae, you don't get it. Your mom died and I'm sorry about that, but she's not around. My mom is. I know some stuff about this. And one thing I know is you have to believe. You have to dig in. She never talks about it, but there are things I've picked up... you have to act. Fate requires motion. That's why the guy has to find your offering and bring it back. He has to know you belong. He gives it back and he trusts that you'll accept it, and that act of faith ties you together."

"But we don't even know for certain if the offerings are there."

"Yes, we do. I believe," Josie said quietly. "Do you?"

Her shift in tone stilled the panic inside me and suddenly, I could feel the truth deep in my bones.

"Yes."

Josie gave me a small, tough smile.

"Then I'm going."

"No. You're not." I put a hand on her arm. "I don't think you can complete the task. I think you'll fall. My dream as much as said so. I'll be fine. You won't. So sit your stubborn butt down. How's that for total honesty?"

"It's a little mean." Josie grinned.

"This is why you like her?" Kate snarled. We ignored her.

"It's my vision. I'll go," I said.

Before she could stop me, before I could stop myself, I climbed up on the beam.

"Fate requires action," I told myself. "You can't control what happens. Summer goes, then seasons change. It's your reaction that matters. It's how you rise to the challenge you face."

"Enough with the feel-good mantras," Josie complained.

"If I'm gonna die, I get my say," I shot right back. But I took a breath, then stepped out on the ledge.

The first steps were easy.

Near the side of the barn, I could hold a crossbeam for support.

I made my way forward inch by inch until the negotiation became more difficult.

About four feet away from the loft floor, the crossbeams disappeared.

From that point on, it was twenty feet across with no handholds, no crossbars, no bracing or support. Just a six-inch-wide beam and a forty-foot drop. Should I stumble to break my fall, I saw the collection of rusted farm machinery on the floor from a terrifying new angle.

The distance looked impossible.

But to get to the rooster perch, I'd have to cross.

"You can do it," Josie told me.

"No you can't," Kate singsonged her reply.

I ignored them both and focused on my breath.

"Yes, I can," I told myself.

I breathed deeply and took my first step without the supports.

"Just watch where you're going. Nothing to it. One foot after the other. Walk a straight line." Josie made it sound easy.

I raised my eyeline to the rooster's nest and took a second step.

My balance held.

Keeping the rest of my body as still as possible, I inched across the beam.

"You're almost there!" Josie cheered me on.

"Don't look down," Kate teased.

I couldn't help myself.

I looked.

"Oh god."

The concrete floor zoomed in and out of focus. My knees went weak, and I started to shake. My whole body began to wobble.

I couldn't hold it.

With all my momentum, I flung myself the last few steps and lunged at the rooster's perch for safety. My legs gave way and I dropped from the sky.

"You did it!" Josie celebrated.

Kate politely applauded.

"You didn't die. Way to go."

I opened my eyes.

They were right.

I did it.

When I fell, I landed safely on the perch.

I had made it to the other side of the barn.

The window to the outside world gave a stunning view of the farmland. From this vantage, I could see for miles. It was a beautiful sight of rolling hills.

The sky was starting to brighten, signaling the moment before dawn.

We didn't have much time.

Quickly, I felt around in the hay.

"I got them!"

I dug my anklet out of the straw, and beside it was Josie's delicate watch with its tiny cat ears. I snapped Grandma Mim's necklace back around my own neck for safekeeping but wondered what to do with Josie's timepiece. I thought about putting it around my wrist to travel the distance back across when Kate started to laugh.

"We got back our stuff. What's so funny?" Josie demanded.

"Mae got her offering. She was successful, but you're here with me. I guess we'll start the new coven on our own."

She was right.

The sun was breaking.

The first lick of light was only moments away.

"Run!" Josie shouted.

"I'll never make it. Here!"

Without thinking, I balled her precious offering

into my fist and hurled it across the expanse of the barn.

Josie moved to the edge of the loft to catch it.

"No!"

Kate leapt off the ledge in an attempt to intercept, launching her body through the air in front of Josie's outstretched arms. But she missed.

Josie closed her hand around her watch just as the sun burst over the horizon. It flooded the barn with warm morning light.

On her way down, Kate frantically grabbed the beam I'd just walked across. Her fingers scrabbled on the wood.

"Help me!" she screamed.

"Hold on!" I shouted, making my way back across the beam.

Josie rushed to her aid from the opposite direction.

But Kate hadn't fixed a proper hold on the wood.

Her momentum was too strong.

It continued to carry her.

"No!"

I screamed as her fingertips lost their grip.

In slow motion, Kate slipped from the beam and fell through the air.

Both Josie and I gasped.

Kate's arms pinwheeled, reaching out for supports that just weren't there. Her legs sprawled out from under her. Her hair whipped around her twisted mouth as she screamed. Her eyes bugged out of her head in fear.

The ground rushed up to greet her.

Both Josie and I turned away before the sickening crash. Her body hit the floor.

"Oh god. Get help," I said.

Helpless, I knelt down in the perch.

"Get... somebody."

"I'll get a doctor," Josie said.

She fumbled with her phone.

She put the watch safely back on her wrist as she reported the accident.

The operator asked lots of questions, and soon we could hear sirens in the distance.

Josie made her way back down the ladder.

I sunk to the floor of the small perch.

We'd both recovered our offerings, the things we'd arrived so intent to return. We had our stuff back. But it seemed so insignificant now.

Josie stayed on the phone as she climbed down to barn level to see for herself, but from both of our vantage points, her near and me far, we could see that Kate was gone. A pool of blood seeped out from under her body and dripped down the old farming machinery that had broken her fall.

Josie reached Kate's side and looked up at me.

She shook her head.

She confirmed what I already knew.

Kate was gone.

Josie went out of the barn to wait for the paramedics.

I didn't blame her. I too looked away from the grisly scene.

Back in the safety of the roost, I sank into the straw and looked out the window, over the view of the farmland.

The morning had come.

I should have been mad at Kate, or happy she was gone.

After all, she'd forced us into this position.

With every turn, she'd made poor and dangerous choices. Even in this final showdown, she'd laughed and egged us on. But when I thought of the picture of my mom and her friends laughing and hugging in the photo, Kate, or Kate's mom, or whoever it was... she wasn't part of that embrace. She stood deep in the background, all alone.

Yes, she took our offerings, but Kate's only real crime was being desperate to belong.

THIRTY-THREE
AN INVITATION

JOSIE and I sat together for Kate's funeral.

No one else dared even sit in our pew. We were both celebrities and pariahs in town. Everyone in Plumpkin knew we'd been at the barn when it happened. From the whispers I'd heard, most people chalked it up to a sleepover dare gone horribly wrong.

Josie and I went back to being silent compatriots, both glad to sit by the other, neither with much to say, but happy for the protection the partnership held.

Spade and I were over.

He wouldn't even look in my direction. Since the deadline to parabond had passed, he had no more use for me. It was time for him to realign to his new life without the hope of the High Council.

That was fine.

I had nothing to say to him either.

Aunt Abeline had started floating the idea of another move. Nothing definite, just passing phrases here and there that implied our stay in Plumpkin was no longer permanent. I had a feeling once this semester's exams were over, it would be only a matter of time.

Things were good between Beck and Josie, but anytime she hung out with me, Beck was never around.

I spent a lot of time in the basement hideaway.

Now that the fall weather was really upon us, the downstairs bunker felt cozy and warm. I'd even started sleeping in the underground bedroom. The hideout felt more like home than anywhere else in Plumpkin. It was the one place in the whole town where the truth felt real.

I bought a copy of the previous year's yearbook at the school office and on the day of her burial, I cut out all the pictures of Kate I could find.

I wanted a keepsake.

I could have taken the photo from her funeral memorial program—it was beautiful and elegant—but that seemed too morbid and sad.

No, I wanted to remember her from her moments of living.

She appeared in the yearbook seven times, which was a lot, even for the most popular of kids. Always, she was smiling.

I cut out each snapshot and glued them into an empty page at the back of Mom's photo album. I printed her name very neatly and properly dated her birth to her death. It felt very important to know that she would be accurately remembered.

Once I finished my collage, I put the album back on the shelf.

Strangely, as I did, a white envelope fell out.

That was weird.

I had been through the whole album many, many times, page by page. Before today, there had never been a letter lodged in its span.

I bent down to pick up the letter.

The back of the envelope had a green seal made of hot wax with arrows pointing in opposite directions.

It was addressed to me.

There was no stamp.

Carefully, I slid a nail along the thin glued edge that separated the lid from the envelope. Inside was a single folded paper. I opened it, exposing an exquisitely detailed letterhead also boasting the double arrowhead design.

Slowly, I read:

Dear Mae,

It is with great pleasure we wish to extend to you a cordial invitation to the Judicial Studies of the High Council.

While the circumstances of your entry were not the typical mode of welcome, by a vote of six to one, the High Council has agreed to include you in this year's class. Studies commence on the 17th of the month. Entrance to the school can be found at 128 Wiltonshire Road.

Please be packed to begin your semester abroad.

Many congratulations,
  Cornelius Child
  Fellow Black, Esteemed Headmaster
  Judicial Studies of the High Council

I lowered the page and examined it once more.

How did the envelope get in here?

I alone had the key to our secret basement, and on my way down today, I had to move the guest bedroom rug out of the way.

No one had been in the bunker since I'd returned home from the funeral.

This was an admissions letter to the High Council? But why?

I hadn't... no one found my offering.

Did this mean I'd succeeded in parabonding with myself?

And "prepare for your studies abroad"? What did that mean?

Where were they going?

I didn't even know if joining the High Council was something I still wanted.

The obsession to join the coven had cost Kate her life.

Rolling the letter over and over in my hands, I ascended the staircase back to the lake house. As I floated through the rooms, lost in thought, Aunt Abeline heard me coming. She looked up from our Scrabble game, munching on a spoon-sized nibble of the dinner she was preparing. She pulled the cutlery out of her mouth.

"Mmm. Don't laugh. I could only get fifteen points for *harmful*. I have terrible letters. It's your turn."

She fluttered back to the stove.

"What do you think about moving back to the city?" she wondered. "Someplace so loud and artsy-artsy we can barely hear ourselves think?"

She was making mac and cheese again, my favorite dinner.

No bacon this time though.

Without bad news, she didn't feel the need to sweeten the pot.

"I don't think I can," I told her.

"Oh, sure. Your credits can transfer," she scoffed.

With a casual hand, she waved through the air.

"I think they already did."

I held up the acceptance letter.

"Aunt Abeline, I got in."

WHAT NOW?

Want to dig into sneak peeks, learn about the next releases and find all the other freebies and literary goodies? Join my newsletter at www.juliecatherineau thor.com.

Xo
 Julie

ACKNOWLEDGMENTS

Thank you for spending time with me, Mae, Josie, Beck, Spade and all the other parabond participants. This story has been a big challenge for me as I've created a far bigger world in these chronicles than in any of my previous stories before. Not to worry though, I've loved every minute of it.

Thank you to my editor, Katie Wolf. I was worried about bringing professional feedback into the mix, but boy, am I glad I did. Your tips and suggestions always elevate the words.

Thank you to Allana Giesbrecht, David Guthrie, and Lindsay Taaffe for your input.

My goal writing this series was to create a world where someone might like to live for a while or at least happily visit, taking the time to peep into the trials and tribulations of other people's lives, living with their successes and their troubles and of course exploring a few potential romantic entanglements too.

I hope you'll find the journey fun, exciting, emotional and just a tiny bit magical.

When you're finished *Paranormal Bonds*, I hope you'll consider writing a review on store sites, reader hubs and/or whatever social media platform where you happily hang your hat. Reviews are so important to help authors become visible on the busy, busy landscape. I appreciate each review, ratings, and/or social media share more than I can express.

I am happy to report, Mae's adventures are only beginning and you'll see plenty of return characters as the story unfolds in book 2, *Predetermined Bonds*. See you there!

Xo
    Julie

My Book

The High Council Witch Chronicles

Paranormal Bonds

Predetermined Bonds

Poisoned Bonds

Planted Bonds

Paternal Bonds

The High Council Witch Chronicles prequels

Enchanted Bonds (a prequel novella)

GRAB

your free ebook copy

a prequel novella

get yours at
www.juliecatherineauthor.com